The New York Times

IN THE HEADLINES

Cyberbullying

A DEADLY TREND

THE NEW YORK TIMES EDITORIAL STAFF

Published in 2019 by New York Times Educational Publishing in association with The Rosen Publishing Group, Inc.
29 East 21st Street, New York, NY 10010

First Edition

The New York Times
Alex Ward: Editorial Director, Book Development
Phyllis Collazo: Photo Rights/Permissions Editor
Heidi Giovine: Administrative Manager

Rosen Publishing
Megan Kellerman: Managing Editor
John Giacobello: Editor
Greg Tucker: Creative Director
Brian Garvey: Art Director

Cataloging-in-Publication Data
Names: New York Times Company.
Title: Cyberbullying : a deadly trend / edited by the New York Times editorial staff.
Description: New York : New York Times Educational Publishing, 2019. | Series: In the headlines | Includes glossary and index.
Identifiers: ISBN 9781642821055 (library bound) | ISBN 9781642821062 (pbk.) | ISBN 9781642821079 (ebook)
Subjects: LCSH: Cyberbullying—Juvenile literature. | Cyberbullying—Prevention—Juvenile literature.
Classification: LCC HV6773.15.C92 C93 2019 | DDC 302.34'302854678—dc23

Manufactured in the United States of America

On the cover: Cyberbullying affects people of all ages, and because factors can vary so much from case to case, it's often unclear how individual incidents should be handled; C.J. Burton/ Corbis NX/Getty Images.

Contents

7 Introduction

CHAPTER 1

The Digital Schoolyard

10 More Teens Victimized by Cyber-Bullies BY TARA PARKER-POPE

12 When the Bullies Turned Faceless BY CHRISTOPHER MAAG

17 Survey Exposes Prevalence of Online Harassment BY NICK WINGFIELD

20 Defining Bullying Down BY EMILY BAZELON

23 In the Fight Against Bullying, a Glimmer of Hope BY PERRI KLASS, M.D.

CHAPTER 2

High-Profile Cases

27 Bieber Fights Cyberbullies, but It Wasn't His Idea BY DANIELLA SILVA

29 Curt Schilling Off Little League Broadcasts After 'Unacceptable' Tweet BY RICHARD SANDOMIR

31 Ex-Dolphin Jonathan Martin Is Detained After Social Media Post Shuts School BY KEN BELSON

33 Hackers Publish Nude Pictures on Leslie Jones's Website BY KATIE ROGERS AND JONAH ENGEL BROMWICH

36 Harassed Online, She Remains Determined to Enlist in the Marines BY DAVE PHILIPPS

41 How Do You Stop Bullying? Advertisers Try to Help BY MARTHA C. WHITE

45 Monica Lewinsky Is Back, but This Time It's on Her Terms BY JESSICA BENNETT

56 Monica Lewinsky Breaks Her Public Silence With a TED Talk BY JESSICA BENNETT

59 The Ornithologist the Internet Called a Murderer BY KIRK WALLACE JOHNSON

66 The Rise of the Internet Fan Bully BY AMANDA HESS

CHAPTER 3

Technology Evolves

70 Can Bots Fight Bullying? BY ANNA NORTH

72 A Founder of Secret, the Anonymous Social App, Is Shutting It Down BY MIKE ISAAC

76 Secret's Doomed Script BY JOE NOCERA

79 Who Spewed That Abuse? Anonymous Yik Yak App Isn't Telling BY JONATHAN MAHLER

89 Spying on College Life, via Yik Yak BY LORI ROZSA

92 In Rise of Yik Yak App, Protests and Ethics Collide BY WILLIAM D. COHAN

96 The Rise and Fall of Yik Yak, the Anonymous Messaging App BY VALERIYA SAFRONOVA

103 Name-Calling in the Virtual Playground BY NICK BILTON

106 An App Combats Bullying, One Anonymous Compliment at a Time BY STACY SUAYA

108 Found on Facebook: Empathy BY TEDDY WAYNE

112 Instagram Unveils a Bully Filter BY LAURA M. HOLSON

114 Girl's Suicide Points to Rise in Apps Used by Cyberbullies BY LIZETTE ALVAREZ

118 Meet Facebook's Mr. Nice BY NICK BILTON

CHAPTER 4

Parenting and Education

121 Letting Your Kids Play in the Social Media Sandbox BY NICK BILTON

125 When Your Child Is the Cyberbully BY TARA PARKER-POPE

129 As Bullies Go Digital, Parents Play Catch-Up BY JAN HOFFMAN

142 A Curriculum to Strengthen Students Against Cyberbullying BY VIJAI SINGH

144 Online Bullies Pull Schools Into the Fray BY JAN HOFFMAN

159 Warily, Schools Watch Students on the Internet BY SOMINI SENGUPTA

163 Questions for School on Bullying and a Suicide BY ERIK ECKHOLM AND KATIE ZEZIMA

168 Melania Trump Wants to End Online Bullying. Her Husband Doesn't Help. BY KATIE ROGERS

174 Melania Trump Rolls Out 'Be Best,' a Children's Agenda With a Focus on Social Media BY KATIE ROGERS

CHAPTER 5

Cyberbullying and the Law

179 Charges Dropped in Cyberbullying Death, but Sheriff Isn't Backing Down BY LIZETTE ALVAREZ

184 Private Moment Made Public, Then a Fatal Jump BY LISA W. FODERARO

188 Christie Signs Tougher Law on Bullying in Schools BY RICHARD PÉREZ-PEÑA

190 Jury Finds Spying in Rutgers Dorm Was a Hate Crime BY KATE ZERNIKE

195 Rutgers Webcam-Spying Defendant Is Sentenced to 30-Day Jail Term BY KATE ZERNIKE

200 When Neighbors Tangle Online BY RONDA KAYSEN

208 Glossary
210 Media Literacy Terms
213 Media Literacy Questions
215 Citations
220 Index

Introduction

BULLYING IS NOT NEW. Cruelty, abuse and public humiliation have always been unfortunate aspects of human life in some form. But all are rapidly intertwining with technology as it evolves, as social media's grip on culture tightens and as the protective boundaries between private selves and public personae seem to dissolve. Privacy issues that were until recently restricted to celebrities now concern the most anonymous among us. The result has been a kind of Information Age vertigo.

Sadly, young people are the most deeply impacted. Many parents and educators feel helpless in the face of these developments, caught between encouraging children and young adults to immerse themselves in the many benefits of technological innovation, and trying to protect them from the profound damage this same innovation makes possible.

Not long ago a natural human optimism seemed to guide our initial approach to the Internet revolution. Throughout its inception, the miracle of the "Information Superhighway" was understandably difficult for most to behold with anything short of wonder, while concerns about what may lurk down its darker streets were often dismissed as technophobia. This helped maintain the momentum of countless important developments, from now-commonplace conveniences like online shopping and streaming music, to seismic shifts in politics and social justice. Marginalized groups gained a platform unheard of among past generations of activists.

Meanwhile, cyberbullies and malicious hackers crept from those forgotten dark streets and into the mainstream of our daily lives on the same momentum, leaving us mourning our casualties and scrambling for solutions. Human optimism is tested as we face our most negative habits and tendencies, now enhanced with the use of digital steroids.

STUART BRADFORD

Fortunately many among us are searching for new ways to fight. Monica Lewinsky, possibly the first well-known victim of extreme online harassment, encourages us in a viral campaign to "Click With Compassion." Lewinsky maintains that in our online world, clicks are currency, and the less currency provided to negative posts, the less power they can wield. New apps like Brighten, developed by Austin Kevitch, encourage compliments as an alternative to snark. Other apps such as Secret and Yik Yak, widely associated with bullying and gossip, are now defunct due in part to public opposition. High-profile cyber harassment incidents involving celebrities and popular sports teams, however painful for the parties involved, have raised awareness and increased public communication on the issue.

Technology itself is also being creatively deployed to counter online abuse. Instagram, one of the most popular social networks, took a stand against bullying in 2017 with a tool called DeepText. The algorithm tracks down harassing comments in ways more advanced than standard filters used previously. Another new tool called Conversation AI, developed by Google subsidiary Jigsaw, uses artificial intelligence to recognize harassing language and even consider its context.

While these developments are encouraging and important, cyberbullying's apparent consequences continue, the most tragic and extreme among them being suicide. The link between cyberbullying and suicide can be difficult to prove legally, even in cases where the harasser in literal terms encourages the victim to kill themselves. Why a human being would encourage another to end their life falls beyond the scope of technology and may never adequately be answered. And that mystery may well be the most urgent incentive to bring as much awareness and understanding to the issue as humanly possible.

CHAPTER 1

The Digital Schoolyard

Just as technology has drastically changed the face of education, it has just as powerfully changed the way students relate to one another. This chapter looks at the ways that online communication can make abuse and cruelty easier for young people to inflict on their peers.

More Teens Victimized by Cyber-Bullies

BY TARA PARKER-POPE | NOV. 27, 2007

THE SCHOOLYARD BULLY has gone digital.

As more and more young people have access to computers and cell phones, a new risk to teens is beginning to emerge. Electronic aggression, in the form of threatening text messages and the spread of online rumors on social networking sites, is a growing concern. Researchers estimate that between 9 percent and 34 percent of youth are victims of so-called "cyber-bullies." And as many as one out of five teens has bullied another youth using digital media, reports a special issue of the Journal of Adolescent Health.

Although the majority of kids who are harassed online aren't physically bothered in person, the cyber-bully still takes a heavy emotional toll on his or her victims. Kids who are tormented online are more likely to get a detention or be suspended, skip school and experience emotional distress, the medical journal reports. Teens who receive rude or nasty comments via text messages are six times more likely to say they feel unsafe at school.

The concern is that bullying is still perceived by many educators and parents as a problem that involves physical contact. Most research and enforcement efforts focus on bullying in school classrooms, locker rooms, hallways and bathrooms. But given that 80 percent of adolescents use cell phones or computers, "social interactions have increasingly moved from personal contact at school to virtual contact in the chat room," write Kirk R. Williams and Nancy G. Guerra, researchers at the University of California, Riverside and co-authors of one of the journal reports. "Internet bullying has emerged as a new and growing form of social cruelty."

Cyber-bullying tactics include humiliation, destructive messages, gossip, slander and other "virtual taunts" communicated through e-mail, instant messaging, chat rooms and blogs.

School districts in Florida, South Carolina, Utah and Oregon have responded by creating new policies to deal with digital bullies. New York City is enforcing rules banning communication devices in school buildings, and Washington State recently passed a law requiring that cyber-bullying be part of school district harassment prevention policies.

When the Bullies Turned Faceless

BY CHRISTOPHER MAAG | DEC. 16, 2007

DARDENNE PRAIRIE, MO. — Like most mobs, the one that pursued Megan Meier was cruel and unrelenting. Its members gathered on the social networking site MySpace and called Megan a liar, a fat whore and worse.

Megan, 13, fought back, insulting her tormenters with every profanity she knew. But the mob shouted her down, overwhelming her computer and her shaky self-confidence with a barrage of hateful instant messages.

"Mom, they're being horrible!" Megan said, sobbing into the phone when her mother called. After an hour, Megan ran into her bedroom and hanged herself with a belt.

"She felt there was no way out," Ms. Meier said.

Megan Meier's suicide made headlines because she was the victim of a hoax. Lori Drew, another mother in the neighborhood, said in a police report that she had created a MySpace profile of a boy, an invention named "Josh Evans," and that she and her daughter had manipulated Megan into thinking that this fabricated person liked her.

Then, after a few weeks, Ms. Meier said, girls posing as Josh wrote MySpace messages telling Megan that he hated her. He insulted her, and other girls — most unaware that Josh did not exist — viciously piled on. (Later, through her lawyer, Ms. Drew, 48, denied creating the MySpace page used in the hoax and denied knowledge of the final messages.)

In some ways, the hoax was a tragic oddity. Most mothers don't pull vicious pranks, and few harassed adolescents become depressed and commit suicide. But Megan's story is also a case study about cyberbullying.

Cellphone cameras and text messages, as well as social networking Web sites, e-mail and instant messaging, all give teenagers a wider range of ways to play tricks on one another, to tease and to intimidate their peers.

And unlike traditional bullying, which usually is an intimate, if highly unpleasant, experience, high-tech bullying can happen anywhere, anytime, among lots of different children who may never actually meet in person. It is inescapable and often anonymous, said sociologists and educators who have studied cyberbullying.

Even in this town, where Megan's name is a constant reminder of the danger of the Web, adolescents say they love using the technology — and some do a little bullying of their own.

"I'm sure that every girl at this table has used cellphones or instant messaging to say something mean about somebody," said Victoria Fogarty, as she discussed bullying with six other adolescents. Victoria, 14, is the daughter of Pam Fogarty, the mayor of Dardenne Prairie, and an eighth grader at West Middle School, which Megan attended.

Other children are afraid of becoming the next victim.

"Once you're on MySpace, you're trapped," said Jake Dobson, 12, a seventh grader at West Middle School. "You spend all your time online just trying to keep the negative stuff about you from spreading."

Megan Meier spent months begging for a MySpace page before her mother finally gave in. Ms. Meier thought that making friends online could be good for her daughter, a sensitive girl who craved an emotional connection.

But that neediness made Megan vulnerable. By the third grade Megan hated herself and talked of suicide, Ms. Meier said. The diagnosis was depression and attention deficit disorder, which meant Megan would receive weekly counseling and an evolving list of medications as treatment.

By the time she reached seventh grade at West Middle School, Megan was overweight but active, Ms. Meier said. She hung out with other volleyball players, who were in the second tier of popular girls, just beneath the soccer players, said Laura Rodgers, 14, Megan's friend.

She aped the styles of those above her, Ms. Meier said. She favored clothes like Hollister and Abercrombie & Fitch. Sometimes she applied so much mascara that she resembled a raccoon. Occasionally she would gleefully accept a soccer girl's invitation to sit at the popular table during lunch, Laura said.

These moments of success faded during gym class, when Megan had to trade her plus-size designer clothes for athletic shorts and T-shirts. "People in P.E. class called her fat every day," Laura said. "I'd see her in the locker room crying."

After a difficult year, Megan's parents transferred their daughter to Immaculate Conception Catholic School in Dardenne Prairie. The school had strict policies aimed at avoiding cliques. Students wear uniforms, and they are assigned lunch tables so they can socialize with everybody.

"There aren't really cliques there at all," said Rachel Garzon, 14, who befriended Megan. "You might be closer friends with some people, but you can walk up and talk to anybody and they'll be nice to you."

Megan, who had escaped the old cliques, retained her old MySpace page. "She technically wasn't old enough, because you have to be 14," Ms. Meier said. "But I was the only one who knew the password. I read every message she received or sent. I thought I could keep it safe, and Megan could meet some friends."

MySpace uses algorithms and people to strike harassing or bullying images and content, the company said in a written statement, and the site offers users opportunities to report cyberbullies.

But controlling the Web can be almost impossible, experts on children say, and most adolescents are simply not mature enough to handle the virtual world and its anonymous attacks. For instance, "Adolescents take what is said online as the literal truth," said Justin Patchin, assistant professor of criminal justice at the University of Wisconsin, Eau Claire, who studies cyberbullying.

And, as in the Megan Meier case, the victim of cyberbullying is often isolated, yet never free from attack. "The target sees this entire cyberuniverse where everybody is against them, and no one will come to their defense," said Dr. Walter Roberts, professor of counselor education at Minnesota State University, Mankato. "The harassment is not limited to the portion of the day when the kids are in school. The targeted kids have no escape."

Three years ago, before Megan's suicide, the school system identified cyberbullying as a serious problem, said Kim Carter, assistant superintendent for student services in the Fort Zumwalt School District.

In 2005, the school surveyed students and teachers. And before and after Megan's death, the district held a variety of assemblies, meetings and workshops to train students, parents, faculty and administrators how to recognize and react to cyberbullying.

While all the vigilance has helped, students say, cyberbullying remains common. Last month, a girl won $500 in a class raffle. Before her teacher even opened the door to excuse everyone, the rest of the school was abuzz with rumors that she had cheated, said Sarah Fogarty, another of the mayor's children.

How was that possible? Cellphones are supposed to be turned off in school. Girls practice text messaging with their eyes closed, Sarah said. They've become adept at pressing buttons under their desks while keeping their focus on the teacher.

"I'm not good at it yet," Sarah said.

This fall an unpopular boy started break dancing at a football game. People took cellphone photos and videos, which they immediately forwarded to hundreds of people. "They were egging him on because they wanted to keep making fun of him, and the photos made him look ridiculous," said Jake Dobson, the seventh grader.

Even popular kids feel vulnerable.

Ryan Franklin, 12, was a star player on his Little League baseball team until he needed stomach surgery last summer, said his mother, Sonya Franklin. As he recovered, a friend sent e-mail messages to dozens of students falsely stating that Ryan had made sexual comments about a girl in class, Ms. Franklin said.

"The truth was that he'd stopped playing baseball and so he'd lost some of his status," Ms. Franklin said. "Some people started picking on him because he was an easier target." The e-mail messages stopped only when she threatened to call the boy's mother.

Jake Dobson admits he's not above an instant message making fun of someone, even if he knows that the same thing could happen to him.

"It's like I can't even do anything because everybody is sitting there with a cellphone just waiting for me to mess up," he said.

Survey Exposes Prevalence of Online Harassment

BY NICK WINGFIELD | OCT. 22, 2014

AN EXHAUSTIVE NEW STUDY reveals that 40 percent of adult Internet users have personally experienced some form of online intimidation.

The study, by the Pew Research Center, shows the extent to which harassment has affected the online experiences of many people. It provides further insight into a phenomenon that has attracted widespread attention in recent months with the hounding of female video game developers and critics.

Those attacks have included threats of violence, culminating in anonymous emails last week that led one critic, Anita Sarkeesian, to cancel a speech at Utah State University.

The Pew survey of American Internet users attempts to quantify the prevalence of harassment in all its forms, ranging from name-calling and efforts to embarrass others to more extreme behaviors like stalking, making physical threats and sexual harassment. Among people who said they had been harassed online, 55 percent said they experienced it exclusively in milder forms while 45 percent said they were subject to severe varieties of harassment. Of all adult Internet users, 22 percent had experienced mild forms of harassment online, Pew found, and 18 percent had experienced severe forms of harassment.

Nearly three-quarters of Internet users had witnessed someone else being harassed online, Pew found.

Harassment was not invented in the Internet era, but it became easier and had fewer consequences thanks to the many varieties of cheap, anonymous online communications. By far the most common channels for online harassment are social-networking sites and apps, Pew said, with 66 percent of adult Internet users identifying those as the source of harassment.

The group of people Pew surveyed consisted only of adults, which means the findings did not reflect the problem of teenage cyberbullying. In a 2012 survey, Pew found that teenagers were more likely than adults to witness mean and cruel behavior on social-networking sites.

The latest Pew study of harassment comes from a survey of more than 2,800 respondents, with a margin of error of plus or minus 2.4 percentage points.

Half of people who said they had been harassed did not know the person responsible for the most recent episode. Although online intimidation of women has received the most attention lately, men are slightly more likely than women to experience Internet harassment in some form, at 44 percent to 37 percent.

The online abuse directed at women in the game industry has shown how harassment can mushroom into a much broader movement. The invective directed at Ms. Sarkeesian and other women has come after they challenged stereotyping of women in games and other conventions of the medium.

Online games themselves can be troubling conduits for abuse, including sexual harassment. Pew said that 16 percent of people who had experienced harassment, men and women included, said online games were where it occurred most recently.

One person on the receiving end of such abuse was Cindy, one of nearly 1,000 people who responded to a request from The New York Times last week asking readers for their accounts of sexism in the game industry:

> *I work in gaming and I play competitively. Sexism is more apparent when playing as most people can hide behind a monitor and spout off their sexism. I once outplayed a competitor who promptly told me he was going to find out where I lived and rape me because I deserved it.*

In fact, online games stood out in the Pew study for differences in the way men and women are treated in them. While users saw other online environments as equally welcoming to both sexes, 44 percent said online games were more welcoming to men, by far the most in Pew's study.

Defining Bullying Down

OPINION | BY EMILY BAZELON | MARCH 11, 2013

NEW HAVEN — The March 3 death of Bailey O'Neill, a 12-year-old boy in Darby Township, Pa., was widely attributed to bullying, based on allegations that a classmate hit the boy in the face in January. He suffered a concussion, his family said, and eventually seizures.

Bullying was also the headline in the death of Amanda Todd, a 15-year-old Canadian girl who committed suicide after making a viral video in which she described being seduced, stalked and blackmailed online, probably by an adult.

Were these instances of actual bullying? It's hard to say. But what's notable is that observers automatically assumed they were, even though we know that "bullying" isn't the same as garden-variety teasing or a two-way conflict. The word is being overused — expanding, accordionlike, to encompass both appalling violence or harassment and a few mean words. State laws don't help: a wave of recent anti-bullying legislation includes at least 10 different definitions, sowing confusion among parents and educators.

All the misdiagnosis of bullying is making the real but limited problem seem impossible to solve. If every act of aggression counts as bullying, how can we stop it? Down this road lies the old assumption that bullying is a rite of childhood passage. But that's wrong.

Bullying is a particular form of harmful aggression, linked to real psychological damage, both short and long term. There are concrete strategies that can succeed in addressing it — and they all begin with shifting the social norm so that bullying moves from being shrugged off to being treated as unacceptable. But we can't do that if we believe, and tell our children, that it's everywhere.

The definition of bullying adopted by psychologists is physical or verbal abuse, repeated over time, and involving a power imbalance. In other words, it's about one person with more social status lording it over another person, over and over again, to make him miserable.

But when every bad thing that happens to children gets called bullying, we end up with misleading narratives that obscure other distinct forms of harm. In the case of Bailey, the district attorney has said he has found no evidence of bullying as he properly defines it: a history of intimidation over time. It's a tragedy if the evidence ends up showing that he died from head injuries caused by another child's punches, but it's a different kind of tragedy if that child was known for bullying, and that his parents and his school failed to stop him.

In the video Amanda Todd made before her death, her account of online seduction, stalking and blackmail cries out for condemnation and police investigation. Yet because she also reported conflicts with kids at her school, her death was mostly ascribed simply to bullying.

On the other extreme of the spectrum, overly broad legal definitions of bullying — for example, ones that leave out the factors of repetition or power imbalance — can lead parents to cry bully whenever their child has a conflict with another child.

Sorting through the accusations is a burden for schools, especially when state laws straitjacket their response to a bullying accusation, rather than allowing them to use their judgment and take account of context. And the "bully" label carries a stigma that's hard for a child to escape. It makes a child seem permanently heartless, rather than capable of feeling empathy, which almost all are.

Crying wolf about bullying isn't good for the children who play the victim, either. Those who hold onto that identity are less likely to recover from adversity. Bullying victims need sympathy; they also need help learning to be resilient.

One way to better identify real bullying is to listen to how teenagers themselves describe their interpersonal conflicts. Most teenagers can identify bullying, but they can also distinguish it from what they often call "drama," which, the researchers Danah Boyd and Alice Marwick have shown, is an accurate and common name for the ordinary skirmishes that mark most children's lives. In fact, it's drama that's common, and bullying, properly defined, that's less so.

Understanding what bullying means to children is integral to the success of every smart bullying prevention effort, because it harnesses the power of the majority. One effective strategy is for schools to survey their own students about bullying, and then broadcast the results to students. When they see evidence of what most of them know intuitively — that bullying is outlier behavior — they're even less likely to engage in it.

It's also crucial for the adults in the school to set the tone. They have to understand what bullying is and what it's not, respond when they see a domineering child going after a victim, and foster the strong ties with students that make all the difference for children's sense of belonging and decisions about where to turn when they need help.

Adults can also often do more good by asking questions that push children to come up with their own strategies than by dictating solutions themselves. By many measures, teenagers today are faring better than they were a generation ago. The rates of teenage pregnancy, binge drinking and drunken driving are down. So is violent juvenile crime and even fighting on school property.

Those heartening developments help explain why bullying is holding our national attention: as a society, we have the wherewithal now to attend to a psychological harm that has long deeply affected kids, but which adults used to mostly ignore. Bullying is a problem we can and should address. But not if we're wrongly led to believe that it's everything and everywhere.

EMILY BAZELON is a senior editor at Slate and the author of "Sticks and Stones: Defeating the Culture of Bullying and Rediscovering the Power of Character and Empathy."

In the Fight Against Bullying, a Glimmer of Hope

BY PERRI KLASS, M.D. | AUG. 28, 2017

IN RECENT YEARS, educators, pediatricians and parents have worried a great deal about bullying and the effects it can have on children, and the question of whether school programs and policies can make a difference.

A new study suggests that things can indeed get better.

In the study, published in May in the journal Pediatrics, researchers looked at data from 10 years of student surveys about bullying in Maryland schools. They saw a decrease in 10 of the 13 indicators of bullying they were measuring.

Catherine Bradshaw, a professor and associate dean at the University of Virginia and the senior author of the study, has been collaborating with school districts in Maryland for more than a decade, administering a detailed online survey on school climate and bullying to nearly 250,000 students from grade 4 to grade 12. Students were asked whether they had been frequent victims of bullying, or frequent perpetrators, and asked in more detail about physical bullying (pushing and slapping), verbal bullying, relational bullying (spreading rumors), and cyberbullying. They were also asked if they had seen other people being bullied. And finally, they were asked about some attitudes relevant to bullying ("Bullying is a problem at this school," for example), and about feeling safe at school.

Over the period of the study, from 2005 to 2014, students' reports of being bullied in all of those ways decreased, as did reports of perpetrating bullying, and of witnessing bullying. And more students reported feeling safe at school.

So in these Maryland school districts, things were getting better, and the improvement tended to accelerate around 2010. The study did not involve instituting anti-bullying programs, nor did it account for what practices were in place in participating schools. Therefore the researchers could not attribute the improvement to particular programs.

"It's very exciting," Dr. Bradshaw said, "but we need to be very clear that although there is some good news, we're still seeing 20 percent of kids not feeling safe at school. We haven't solved this problem, but it gives us hope that policies and practices may have improved things."

"The Maryland data is a very large sample over 10 years controlling for a number of different variables," said Stephen Leff, a clinical psychologist and co-director of the Violence Prevention Initiative at Children's Hospital of Philadelphia, who was a co-author of a commentary on the study. "It really does provide a unique picture window." On the other hand, he said, this study doesn't really tell us why the behaviors are going down or attempt to measure the impact of the bullying that still goes on.

Cyberbullying in particular, even if the rates are low, "can have such a negative impact," Dr. Leff said, and can do great harm to a whole peer group, or to school culture more generally. "I want to caution schools and parents that it's still quite a problem, its frequency may be down, but the issue and the impact I think is still great."

Dr. Andrew Adesman, the chief of developmental and behavioral pediatrics at Cohen Children's Medical Center of New York, argued in a comment on the Maryland study that these findings are not reflective of national trends. He said that cyberbullying is pandemic among high school students. The Maryland data, he said in an email, "include some high school students but mostly younger students, and while it is encouraging that these rates are decreasing in Maryland, that may not reflect what is happening nationally among high school students."

Dr. Adesman cited data from the Centers for Disease Control and Prevention's Youth Risk Behavior Surveillance System which showed no overall decrease in the prevalence of high school students being bullied on school property in recent years, though the same survey did show a decrease among Maryland high school students.

He also stressed the danger of bullying and the damage it can do, particularly cyberbullying, which he said has "amplified the impact, morbidity and the potential mortality." The ramifications of cyberbullying, he said, can go well beyond the moment, because what is posted online can hang around in cyberspace and can so easily spread to include more people. "It is estimated that 20 percent of suicides in teens and young adults are due to bullying, and suicide is one of the leading causes of death in this age range," he said in an email.

A 2014 analysis published in JAMA Pediatrics examined data from many studies and concluded that bullying was linked to both suicidal thoughts and suicide attempts, with cyberbullying most likely to be linked to suicidal thoughts and behavior.

Bullying remains a tremendously important issue for parents to be aware of, and the online side of bullying is as dangerous to adolescents as it is opaque to many parents; there is an excellent federal government website on bullying, and a helpful set of information for parents on cyberbullying available as well from Common Sense media.

"Take it seriously if your child tells you they're being bullied online or with text messages," Dr. Leff said. "Don't as a response take away the technology." Doing that may make children less likely to tell adults when cyberbullying is going on, and it won't change the behaviors or the emotions. Instead, parents should open lines of communication and talk this through.

In talking with parents who are concerned about a child who has reported being bullied, Dr. Leff said, "it's always important as a parent to stay calm, to be able to listen, to be able to hear about the situation calmly, not reacting emotionally." This is no easy assignment, he acknowledged.

Parents need to get the facts, he said, and understand whether what has taken place is really bullying, which is generally defined as repeated use of aggression physically, socially or electronically, in the context of a power imbalance. Ask questions. Get the child to describe what happened and what led up to it, where it happened and how long it has been happening.

And then, Dr. Leff said, he and his colleagues advise parents to reach out to the school, but not to directly contact the parents of the bully.

"What we often tell parents is set up a meeting with the principal, stay calm — then to find a point person at the school that their child can talk to when there's a problem." Parents should ask for a plan in writing as to how the situation is going to be addressed, and how the school is going to monitor what is going on.

"I think the main message is there's room for some optimism, we are really better understanding what works and how it matches the needs of the school," Dr. Leff said. "But there's still way too many kids being bullied physically as well as socially and electronically."

The school programs that have demonstrated the greatest impact in other studies, cited in Dr. Leff's commentary, are whole-school approaches that involve students, teachers and parents, which may help students develop skills in problem-solving and empathy and learn to be "positive bystanders."

But such programs work only when properly implemented, so schools need to find programs that match their needs. If the decrease seen in Maryland is at least in part a result of effective antibullying programs in schools, it becomes even more important to help schools choose the right programs.

"We haven't solved this problem," Dr. Leff said, "but it gives us hope that policies and practices may have improved things."

CHAPTER 2

High-Profile Cases

As news of cyberbullying spreads, more well-known figures are becoming involved. Some are joining the fight against online cruelty; many are its victims. Some could even be classified as cyberbullies themselves. Nobody, regardless of age or social status, is immune. This chapter examines some of the ways popular culture is being shaped by this issue at varying levels.

Bieber Fights Cyberbullies, but It Wasn't His Idea

BY DANIELLA SILVA | OCT. 10, 2012

JUSTIN BIEBER STARS in a new video that was released on Wednesday, but the inspiration did not come from him. Instead, it came from a prosecutor.

Mr. Bieber, who enjoys a huge teenage fan base, made the video, warning of the dangers of cyberbullying, as part of a plea agreement with the Nassau County district attorney that resolved charges against one of Mr. Bieber's managers and a record company executive.

The charges against the manager, Scott Braun, and the executive, James Roppo, stemmed from a crowd-control episode in 2009 at the Roosevelt Field shopping mall in Nassau County.

In 2009, Mr. Bieber was scheduled to sign autographs at the mall. But when more than 3,000 young fans converged there before his arrival, the police ordered the event to be canceled for safety reasons.

The police said a message from Mr. Bieber's Twitter account hindered their attempts to disperse the crowd. The message said, "On my way to Roosevelt Field Mall in Long Island, NY to sign and meet fans! I'm pumped. See u there."

The police said they asked Mr. Bieber's employees to send another Twitter message from Mr. Bieber's account to say the event was canceled. But employees at Island Records, Mr. Bieber's label, were unable to do so because, the police said, Mr. Braun had changed the account's password.

Mr. Braun did eventually send two Twitter messages canceling the event, and the crowd dispersed.

Mr. Braun and Mr. Roppo were charged with misdemeanors for failing to immediately cooperate with the police.

Kathleen M. Rice, the Nassau County district attorney, said the video was made as part of a criminal settlement with Mr. Bieber's management companies.

The companies also agreed to plead guilty to fire code violations and paid Nassau County $24,000, according to a news release.

"I saw an opportunity for something innovative that would be a much larger benefit to the community than the companies just paying a few hundred dollars in fines," Ms. Rice said in a statement explaining the Bieber video. "Unusual cases often require innovative solutions and I think we were able to find one here."

The video, which is available on YouTube, will be featured on a new Web site created by the district attorney's office and will be distributed on DVD to Nassau County schools.

A spokeswoman for Mr. Bieber did not immediately respond on Wednesday afternoon to an e-mail or a telephone call.

Curt Schilling Off Little League Broadcasts After 'Unacceptable' Tweet

BY RICHARD SANDOMIR | AUG. 25, 2015

CURT SCHILLING, the ESPN "Sunday Night Baseball" analyst and former major league pitcher, was pulled from calling a Little League World Series game Tuesday night because of a post he shared on his Twitter account that suggested extremist Muslims were comparable to Nazis. The post featured an image of Adolf Hitler.

Although he has been contributing to ESPN's Little League World Series coverage, Tuesday night's broadcast was to be his first as a game analyst.

"Curt's tweet was completely unacceptable, and in no way represents our company's perspective," ESPN said in a statement. "We made that point very strongly to Curt and have removed him from his current Little League assignment pending further consideration."

Schilling quickly deleted the post and apologized on Twitter, saying: "I understand and accept my suspension. 100% my fault. Bad choices have bad consequences and this was a bad decision in every way on my part."

Robert O. Trestan, the New England director of the Anti-Defamation League, said in a statement that "we are glad that he realized how his tweet offended Muslims and Jews," but added that the analogy he made has "no place in civil debate."

"As horrible as the acts committed by Islamic extremists are, comparing this to state-controlled genocide committed by the Nazis is disgusting," Trestan said.

No ESPN officials were available to say if they would impose further discipline on Schilling.

Schilling is the second on-air personality reprimanded by ESPN in recent days. Cris Carter, an N.F.L. studio analyst, was found in a

2014 rookie symposium video to have advised young players to "have a fall guy in your crew" if any of them found himself in legal trouble.

"We completely disagree with his remarks and we have made that extremely clear to him," ESPN said in a statement. Carter apologized, saying, "I can't make an excuse for what my mind-set was."

Schilling is active on Twitter and Facebook, where his accounts are filled with baseball talk, biblical references, pro-military and anti-abortion messages, and conservative political statements that are frequently punctuated by sharing memes. On Facebook, he has numerous photographs of Nazi and Third Reich memorabilia that are parts of his World War II collection.

Months ago, he said that he had started selling some of it "due to space issues."

Earlier this year, he used the Internet to aggressively protect his daughter, Gabby, from vulgar comments posted by cyberbullies on Twitter. In defending his actions, he wrote on his blog about himself: "I have a nasty habit of talking, a lot, about anything anyone asks me and totally unconcerned about giving you my opinion. You will never question where I stand, right or wrong agree or disagree on anything."

He is also known for the bankruptcy in 2012 of his video game company, 38 Studios, that left Rhode Island taxpayers liable for the bonds it had issued to help him expand.

Schilling, 48, joined ESPN in 2010 and was added as a "Sunday Night Baseball" analyst in late 2013. Before the 2014 season, he was found to have mouth cancer that he said had been caused by chewing tobacco. In a letter to his younger self posted this year on The Players' Tribune, Schilling wrote: "You will develop sores, you will lose your sense of taste and smell. You will develop lesions. You will lose your gums — they will rot. You will have problems with your teeth for the rest of your life."

Ex-Dolphin Jonathan Martin Is Detained After Social Media Post Shuts School

BY KEN BELSON | FEB. 23, 2018

JONATHAN MARTIN, the former N.F.L. offensive lineman who was at the center of a bullying scandal in 2013, was detained by the police after posting a seemingly threatening message on social media.

A photograph he posted on Instagram showed a shotgun and included a message that said bullying victims had only two choices, suicide and revenge. It included the name of the private high school he attended in Los Angeles, prompting officials there to shut the school on Friday.

"When you're a bully victim & a coward, your options are suicide, or revenge," the post read.

The incident comes less than two weeks after a former student at Marjory Stoneman Douglas High School in Parkland, Fla., killed 17 teachers and students.

Officials at Harvard-Westlake School in Los Angeles sent an alert to students around 7 a.m. Friday. Martin, who posted the image on his Instagram account on Thursday, did not explicitly threaten the school. But the photo of the shotgun and shells included the hashtag #HarvardWestlake.

"Out of abundance of caution, and because the safety of our students, faculty, and staff is our top priority, we made the decision to close school today," the school said in a statement. "We are working closely with law enforcement and will share more information when we are able."

Martin's photo also included the hashtag #MiamiDolphins, the team that drafted him out of Stanford in 2012.

In 2013, Martin left the team after seven games because he said that another offensive lineman, Richie Incognito, had repeatedly bullied him and used racist language. Martin left the team abruptly and later said that he was under psychological duress and had considered suicide.

Incognito was suspended for bullying Martin, other teammates and a team employee. Martin played the next season for the San Francisco 49ers, but has not appeared in an N.F.L. game since then.

Incognito sat out the 2014 season, but played the next three years for the Buffalo Bills.

A 144-page report commissioned by the N.F.L. to explore allegations of bullying on the Dolphins found that Incognito and two fellow offensive linemen, John Jerry and Mike Pouncey, "engaged in a pattern of harassment" toward Martin; another young offensive lineman; and an assistant trainer, including improper touching and sexual taunting.

In his post on Instagram on Thursday, Martin included the social media handles for Incognito and Pouncey, among others.

Incognito insisted that he never bullied Martin and was in fact his friend and mentor. Many of the more than 1,000 text messages between Incognito and Martin that were released contained lewd descriptions and profane language that could be viewed as part of a friendship.

But privately, Martin was furious. According to the report, the mistreatment began early in the 2012 season, Martin's rookie year, and the frequency of insults grew after Martin refused to fight back. Incognito, who is white, sometimes made jokes about slavery in the presence of Martin, who is black, the report said.

Hackers Publish Nude Pictures on Leslie Jones's Website

BY KATIE ROGERS AND JONAH ENGEL BROMWICH | AUG. 24, 2016

LESLIE JONES, a co-star of this year's "Ghostbusters" movie who has been besieged in the past month by online abusers who have targeted her appearance and her race, was victimized again on Wednesday when her personal website appeared to have been hacked.

The hackers inserted a picture of the gorilla Harambe on the site, and exposed what appeared to be explicit photos of the actress, along with pictures of her driver's license and a passport, and images of her with stars like Rihanna, Kanye West and Kim Kardashian West.

The website was taken offline after the hack, which was initially reported by TMZ.

An email to a representative for Ms. Jones was not immediately returned on Wednesday.

The website, which had contained information about her comedy career and her past work in film, appeared to have been retooled to display the personal photos and information.

There was no way to independently confirm that the photos were of Ms. Jones and whether the identification documents were real, but the address on the driver's license appeared to correspond with information about Ms. Jones that is available through public records.

Ms. Jones, 48, had spent much of the past month battling online trolls who sent her a stream of racist imagery, pornography and abusive language. She briefly left Twitter, but later returned to tweet about the Rio Olympics.

In the hours after Ms. Jones's site was taken offline, high-profile defenders offered public support.

"These acts against Leslie Jones are sickening," the musician Questlove wrote in a post on Twitter. "It's racist & sexist. It's disgusting. This is hate crimes. This ain't 'kids joshing round.' "

Others, including Paul Feig, the director of the "Ghostbusters" film, the comedian Patton Oswalt and the singer Katy Perry defended the actress on Twitter.

Brendesha Tynes, a professor of education and psychology at the University of Southern California who specializes in social media and cyberbullying, said in an interview that part of what was fueling the attacks against Ms. Jones was a "serious anti-black woman problem in the U.S."

Dr. Tynes noted the criticism levied at the Olympic gymnast Gabby Douglas while she was competing in Rio, and said, "Even the slightest perceived infraction leads people to get bullied."

Ms. Jones herself had stood up for Ms. Douglas while in Brazil.

Sameer Hinduja, the co-director of the Cyberbullying Research Center and a professor of Criminology at Florida-Atlantic University, applauded Ms. Jones for standing up to those who have victimized her over the past several months.

"She was an advocate for others that have been victimized and haven't spoken up, and that has led to more attention, and has, perhaps indirectly, led to policy change on Twitter's part," he said in an interview, referring to the company's taking action against some of the accounts that had hurled racist insults at Ms. Jones.

He added that Ms. Jones's willingness to remain an active social-media presence may have made her a more tempting target for bullies and hackers.

"Some of those that cyberbully attempt to identify something that you're particularly sensitive about, and because they know that it will get under your skin," Dr. Hinduja said. "Or they're just biased and intolerant, as perhaps was the case considering the racial hatred in some of the attacks on Leslie Jones."

Dr. Tynes said that the hack on Wednesday felt particularly harrowing after Ms. Jones had seemed to prevail over those who attacked her earlier this summer, elevating her public presence by using social media sites such as Twitter and Snapchat prolifically during the Olympics.

"I have to say, as a human being, it's heartbreaking," Dr. Tynes said. "As a researcher, I haven't seen in the adolescents I study anything this heinous."

She said that attacks like these could have serious consequences on a victim's mental health, including symptoms of depression and anxiety.

"I'm hoping that people will once again rally behind her, show her love, and hopefully serve as a buffer against some of the potentially negative consequences," Dr. Tynes said. "I'm at a loss for words, but I do know that people will rally behind her once again."

Harassed Online, She Remains Determined to Enlist in the Marines

BY DAVE PHILIPPS | MARCH 14, 2017

THE TROUBLE STARTED months ago for Savannah Cunningham, who had long dreamed of becoming a Marine, when she was deluged with lewd messages online from men and learned that an all-male group of Marines was circulating a nude video of her on Facebook.

New waves of requests and obscene comments about her appearance arrived every time the video, initially obtained from a former boyfriend, and other photos taken from her Instagram account were reposted along with her identity. "It was horrible," Ms. Cunningham, 19, said from her home in Phoenix.

"It was such a creepy invasion of privacy," she added. "They were actively seeking nude images of me, anything they could get their hands on."

Given such a raw view of the worst of Marine culture, many women might have been turned off by the military. But Ms. Cunningham was determined to enlist. She ships off to basic training the first week of April.

"Someone needs to stand up and say this does not represent the values of the Marine Corps," she said. "If not me, then who? Yes, for a long time it was a boys' club, but there needs to be progress."

News of the invitation-only Facebook group behind the harassment, a 30,000-member collection of active-duty Marines and veterans called Marines United, has turned up the heat on the long-simmering problem of how women are treated in the Marine Corps.

The Marine Corps faced blistering questioning on Tuesday from the Senate Armed Services Committee, with members accusing the leadership of failing to take action on an issue they said the corps has known about for years.

CAITLIN O'HARA FOR THE NEW YORK TIMES

Savannah Cunningham, who begins basic training in the Marine Corps in April, was targeted after a nude video of her began to circulate on social media.

"There is no mystery — this has been going on a very long time, it is right in front of you," Senator Kirsten Gillibrand, Democrat of New York, told Marine Corps commanders, citing a 2013 hearing on the cyberbullying of women in the corps. "When you say to us, 'It's got to be different,' that rings hollow."

In contrite and at times introspective testimony, the Marine Corps commandant, Gen. Robert B. Neller, said the online harassment was a symptom of a broader cultural problem that threatens to undermine the foundation of the fighting force. He vowed to punish all who participated, and to work to make the force of 184,000 a more welcoming place for its 15,000 women.

"You've heard it before, but we are going to have to change how we see ourselves and how we treat each other," he told Ms. Gillibrand. "That's a lame answer, but that's all I have right now. And that's on me."

Commanders said of the 30,000 members of Marines United, only about 500 appeared to have gone into folders of nude photos. Investigators were working to build cases on active duty troops it could identify.

But the group's actions in recent days show that it may not be easy to deter. When the original group page was shut down after the news site Reveal uncovered its actions last week, a core group of photo sharers moved to another secret group called MU 2.0. Then, when that was shut down, they moved to one called MU 3.0.

And even as the top enlisted Marine, Sgt. Maj. Ronald L. Green, condemned the group in testimony before Congress last week, members were taunting him online, according to a veteran, James LaPorta, who has been tracking the group's activities.

"There seems to be no regret," Mr. LaPorta said. "They were using racial slurs and talking about getting pictures of his wife."

The group continues to post on anonymous pornography sites. A recent review of images from these sites shows dozens of identifiable women, naked or partly undressed, along with photos of them in uniform.

Thomas Brennan, a Marine veteran and journalist who first reported on the group, said that he had given the names of 55 Marines involved in the photo sharing — including officers ranked as high as major — to investigators six weeks ago, but that there was no sign that any of them had been removed from duty.

A Marine spokesman said he could not comment on the continuing investigation.

The scandal has now spread to the Army and Navy, which are investigating similar photo sharing groups. But for the tens of thousands of women serving in the military, even successful prosecutions may have little effect on the minefield of bias they say they confront.

More than any other branch of the military, the Marine Corps has resisted integrating women. It still trains recruits separately and fails to give women properly fitting body armor, which the Army has provided for years.

GABRIELLA DEMCZUK FOR THE NEW YORK TIMES

From left, Gen. Robert B. Neller, the Marine Corps commandant, Sean J. Stackley, Acting Secretary of the Navy, and Sgt. Maj. Ronald L. Green, the top enlisted Marine, testified during a Senate Armed Services hearing on Capitol Hill on Tuesday.

"Almost every woman I know in the Marines has faced this kind of harassment, and you try to show you are tough enough to ignore it," said Justine Elena, a former Marine captain who served in Afghanistan and now works for "The Daily Show." "But at some point, by ignoring it, you just condone it."

She recalled an instance when fellow Marines took photos of women in the bathrooms on a ship a friend was serving on.

"We need to stand up and say that is not what the Marines is about," she said.

Last week, after hearing of the widespread photo sharing, Ms. Elena set up a fund-raiser called Female Marines United, in which people could show their opposition to Marines United by donating money to support mental health care for Marine veterans.

Ms. Cunningham, who is just a few weeks away from placing her feet on the painted yellow footprints at basic training that are the symbolic first step in becoming a Marine, said that while she had often been torn about how to respond to the online harassment, she had decided that the best response would be to become the best Marine possible.

Always athletic growing up, she made up her mind in high school to join the military, and chose the Marines, she said, because it was the most selective and demanding. She plans to work on a crew loading missiles on Cobra helicopters.

Two years ago, she began working out intensely to prepare — hitting the gym until her arms, which could not do a single pull-up at first, could knock out 14 in a row.

"I wanted to make sure I could do anything male Marines could," she said. "I didn't want anyone to hold me to a lower standard."

Later, she was dating a Marine, and when he was stationed outside of Arizona, she sent him a short strip tease video.

"I don't typically do that stuff," she said. "But for the person you love, you do things to keep a relationship alive."

The video was soon added to the cache of hundreds of photos and videos of active-duty Marines and veterans — filed with the subject's name, rank and place of duty — that is being circulated by Marines United and other groups. Ms. Cunningham was notified by male Marines she knew who were members of the group, and she was eventually given access to view the whole collection.

She pored through the files, searching for women she knew so she could alert them, knowing that their colleagues and commanders could see them.

But while she was horrified by the actions of the group, she said she never equated it with the Marine Corps. She now dates a Marine sergeant and said that most of the male Marines she knew were just as disgusted by the photo sharing as she was. That was what made her stick with her plan to enlist.

"We have to be positive examples of the change we want to see," she said. "Courage, integrity, honor: I want to live those values."

How Do You Stop Bullying? Advertisers Try to Help

BY MARTHA C. WHITE | OCT. 29, 2017

BACK WHEN MOST of the United States got online via dial-up modem, Monica S. Lewinsky learned how the anonymity of the internet can prompt people to be crude and cruel in a way they never would be in real life. Now she is trying to help others who find themselves the target of vitriol.

To mark October as National Bullying Prevention Month, Ms. Lewinsky, along with the advertising agency BBDO and her public relations manager Dini von Mueffling, started an online campaign against cyberbullying that promotes the hashtag #clickwithcompassion and a suite of emojis developed to support victims of online harassment.

"I think it's really kind of opening up this conversation around starting to recognize and de-stigmatize the bullying that's happening both online and offline in many areas," Ms. Lewinsky said. "We're seeing it in academia — and, of course, politics."

And Ms. Lewinsky is not alone in her attempts to bring attention to the topic. The advertising industry is deploying its well-honed powers of persuasion against bullies who have made the leap from school playgrounds to social networks. Burger King, for example, recently released an ad that looked at how many customers would stand up for a "bullied" Whopper Jr. compared with a teenager being bullied in one of its restaurants.

"Before there was an internet, bullying was thought of as a schoolyard activity," said Greg Hahn, chief creative officer at BBDO. "Now it's as prevalent in adult interactions. Something happens online where those rules don't apply anymore."

The impetus to take on bullying is not only altruistic. Social media increasingly has made brands the target of rumors, boycotts and other attacks.

DAMON WINTER/THE NEW YORK TIMES

"The shoot we did was really emotional," Monica S. Lewinsky said of the anti-bullying commercial.

"Now that word of mouth and social are playing such a large role, and more and more consumers have figured out how to use social, they can get on their soapbox," said Allen Adamson, a brand strategy consultant. "The angrier they are, the more effective they are online."

As a result, advertisers have a greater sense of what bullied individuals face — and are learning what kind of communication serves to counter it. "I think maybe more brands, more people, more entities are experiencing it," said Heidi Arthur, the Ad Council's head of campaign development.

These insights have helped shape the conversation around bullying in the past few years, said Ross Ellis, the founder of STOMP Out Bullying, a nonprofit that is promoting the first Wednesday in November as "National Block It Out Day," an anti-cyberbullying initiative.

Five years ago, the Ad Council spearheaded an anti-bullying campaign that targeted parents; today, it speaks directly to bystanders, both kids and adults. The group has homed in on the language used to characterize harassment and abuse to sharpen the focus on what bullying looks like. It now urges people who witness such behavior to intercede.

"Just saying 'bullying' is fairly broad and speaks to you being on one side of it," Ms. Arthur said. "When you can connect it back to specific behaviors, you can have more of those 'aha' moments."

Ms. Lewinsky hopes that her work will help. The campaign's flagship video depicts what would happen if internet trolls confronted their targets in public rather than online.

"There's an online disinhibition effect, where people hiding behind anonymity and a screen will tend to depart from their normal persona," she said.

The video depicts confrontations like one woman mocking another's weight in a cafe, a pedestrian accosting two men with homophobic hate speech and a woman being labeled a terrorist. The perpetrators and targets were played by actors, but the stunned responses of passers-by who intervened were unscripted.

"The shoot we did was really emotional, not only for the actors, but also for the crew," Ms. Lewinsky said. "We all had very strong reactions to ones that hit home in different ways."

Mr. Hahn said the hateful comments the actors used were taken verbatim from social media accounts. "Sadly, it was all too easy to find them," he said.

Of course, advertisers were well versed in navigating unacknowledged or buried emotions long before the advent of the internet, which some experts suggest has made the industry uniquely positioned to take on today's trolls. And if the industry can position its clients at the forefront of this conversation, those brands stand to benefit.

"I think advertising is really a reflection of what's going on in the times," said Val DiFebo, the chief executive of Deutsch in New York. "I think the value proposition is really about creating a contact point with your consumer that's meaningful to them beyond the product that you're selling."

Mr. Adamson noted that attempting to fight bullying through advertising will have to rely on some of the time-tested strategies marketers have long used.

"Most brands have always been sold on an emotional basis," Mr. Adamson said. "People buy a coffee because it says something about who they are. The only way to deal with this is to make people emotionally motivated to say something. Ultimately, if they're going to change behavior, it's not about a rational argument."

Monica Lewinsky Is Back, but This Time It's on Her Terms

BY JESSICA BENNETT | MARCH 19, 2015

MONICA LEWINSKY WAS SITTING in a Manhattan auditorium last month, watching teenage girls perform a play called "Slut." Ms. Lewinsky was in blue jeans and a blazer, her hair pulled out of her face with a small clip. She was wiping away tears.

In the scene, a young woman was seated in an interrogation room. She had been asked to describe, repeatedly, what had happened on the night in question — when, she said, on their way to a party, a group of guy friends had pinned her down in a taxi and sexually assaulted her. She had reported them. Now everyone at school knew, everyone had chosen a side.

"My life has just completely fallen apart," the girl said, her voice shaking. Her parents were in the next room. "Now I'm that girl."

The play concluded, and Ms. Lewinsky fumbled through her purse for a tissue. A woman came and whisked her to the stage.

"Hi, I'm Monica Lewinsky," she said, visibly nervous. "Some of you younger people might only know me from some rap lyrics."

The crowd, made up largely of high school and college women, laughed. "Monica Lewinsky" is the title of a song by the rapper G-Eazy; her name is a reference in dozens of others: by Kanye, Beyoncé, Eminem, Jeezy. The list goes on.

"Thank you for coming," Ms. Lewinsky continued, "and in doing so, standing up against the sexual scapegoating of women and girls."

She walked back to her seat after speaking, and a woman behind her leaned forward. "I saw you, but I didn't realize I was sitting next to Monica Lewinsky," she said.

A line of girls soon approached. "Thank you for being here," said a teenager in a striped shirt and gold hoop earrings. She asked if she could take a photo, and Ms. Lewinsky winced a little, then politely told her no. "I totally understand," the girl said.

When she was asked later about her reaction to the play, Ms. Lewinsky said: "It's really inspiring to hear people bring awareness to this issue. That scene in the interrogation room was hard to watch. One of the things I've learned about trauma is that when you find yourself retriggered, it's helpful to recognize when things are different."

A lot is different for Monica Lewinsky these days, starting with the fact that, until last year, she had hardly appeared publicly for a decade. Now 41, the former White House intern once famously dismissed by the president as "that woman" holds a master's degree in social psychology from the London School of Economics.

She splits time between New York and Los Angeles, where she grew up, and London, and said it's been hard to find work.

Mostly she has embraced a quiet existence: doing meditation and therapy, volunteering, spending time with friends.

DAMON WINTER/THE NEW YORK TIMES

Monica Lewinsky.

But the quiet ended last May, when she wrote an essay for Vanity Fair about the aftermath of her affair with Bill Clinton — the story a result of a years-long relationship with the magazine and its editor, Graydon Carter. (She was first photographed in its pages by Herb Ritts in 1998.)

In the essay, which was a finalist for a 2015 National Magazine Award, she declared that the time had come to "burn the beret and bury the blue dress" and "give a purpose to my past."

That new purpose, she wrote, was twofold: it was about reclaiming her own story — one that had seemed to metastasize — but also to help others who had been similarly humiliated. "What this will cost me," she wrote, "I will soon find out."

It hasn't appeared to cost her, at least not yet. In fact, the opposite has occurred.

Over the last six months, she has made appearances at a benefit hosted by the Norman Mailer Center (she and Mr. Mailer had been friends), at a New York Fashion Week dinner presentation for the designer Rachel Comey, at the Vanity Fair Oscar party and as her friend Alan Cumming's date at an after-party for the Golden Globes. (Mr. Cumming has known her since the 1990s.)

Recently, she took part in an anti-bullying workshop at the Horace Mann School, and joined a feminist networking group. ("I consider myself a feminist with a lowercase 'f,' " she told me. "I believe in equality. But I think I'm drawn to the issues more than the movement.")

Perhaps most interestingly, in October, onstage at a Forbes conference, she spoke out for the first time about the digital harassment (or cyberbullying) that has affected everyone from female bloggers to Jennifer Lawrence to ... her: "I lost my reputation. I was publicly identified as someone I didn't recognize. And I lost my sense of self," she told the crowd.

She just took that declaration one step further on the main stage at TED in Vancouver, British Columbia, on Thursday, where she issued a biting cultural critique about humiliation as commodity. The title of her 18-minute talk (and, perhaps, the line that best sums up her experience), which received a raucous standing ovation: "The Price of Shame."

This is not Monica Lewinsky's first attempt at reinvention. But it's also not the Monica of more than a decade ago: the one who created a handbag line and tried her hand at reality TV.

This iteration is a bundle of contradictions: warm yet cautious. Open yet guarded. Strong but fragile.

She is likable, funny and self-deprecating. She is also acutely intelligent, something for which she doesn't get much credit. But she is also stuck in a kind of time warp over which she has little control.

At 41, she doesn't have many of the things that a person her age may want: a permanent residence, an obvious source of income (she won't comment on her finances), a clear career path.

She is also very, very nervous. She is worried about being taken advantage of, worried her words will be misconstrued, worried reporters will rehash the past.

She is prepared, almost always, for doomsday: the snippet of a quote that might be taken out of context; questions about the Clintons, whom she declines to discuss. "She was burned ... in myriad ways," said her editor at Vanity Fair, David Friend.

Ms. Lewinsky wouldn't call this a reinvention, though. This, she says, is simply the Monica who in spite of the headlines, in spite of the incessant paparazzi-style coverage, "was seen by many, but truly known by few," as she put it on the TED stage.

"This is me," she told me. "This is a kind of evolution of me."

I had approached her after the Vanity Fair essay in part because I was intrigued, but also because I had a tinge of guilt. I had come of age in the Lewinsky era; my first job out of college was at Newsweek, where the story of the reporter who had uncovered the affair — then saw his story leaked to the Drudge Report — was legend.

I distinctly remember my high school self, wide-eyed, poring over the soft-core Starr report with friends.

None of us had the maturity to understand the complexities, or power dynamics, of the president's affair with a young intern. When I was 16, one dominating image of Monica Lewinsky seemed to overshadow all others: slut. Of course, that 22-year-old intern was only a few years older than me.

And so I emailed her. I told her I was interested in her effort to re-emerge, and had been particularly fascinated by the reaction to it, as if there were a kind of public reckoning underway. Feminists who had stayed silent on the first go-round were suddenly defending her, using terms like "slut-shaming" and "media gender bias" to do it.

The late-night host David Letterman was on air expressing remorse over how he had mocked her, asking, in a recent interview with Barbara Walters, "With some perspective, do you realize this is a sad human situation?" Bill Maher said of reading Ms. Lewinsky's piece in Vanity Fair, "I gotta tell you, I literally felt guilty."

And young women were embracing her: rushing up to her after public events, messaging her on social media, asking if they could take selfies. ("Meeting her felt like meeting a pop culture icon," said Amari Leigh, 17, a cast member in the "Slut" play. "It's crazy to think that one thing she did, when she was not that much older than I am now, impacted her whole life.")

"However you felt about the actual event, the way it played out was pretty grotesque," said Rebecca Traister, a senior editor at The New Republic who was just out of college when the Clinton scandal broke and wrote about it later.

Ms. Traister said she was taken aback when she reread her own article: "Whether it's guilt, or sophistication, or thinking a little harder about sexual power dynamics, I think people have started to think: 'Oh right, she probably does have a right to tell her story. And that's a good thing.' "

This time, Ms. Lewinsky appears determined to tell it on her terms. She has a P.R. agent screening requests and approaches media as one may expect: with the caution of a woman who has been raked over the coals.

She has reason to. Just weeks ago, a short interview with the artist Nelson Shanks was published online. In a question about which portrait subject he had found most difficult to capture, Mr. Shanks noted that his painting of Bill Clinton, which hangs in the National Portrait Gallery, had a shadow as a metaphor for Ms. Lewinsky — created from the shadow of an actual blue dress he had placed on a mannequin. The piece posted on a Sunday. By the next morning, it was everywhere.

Ms. Lewinsky woke up to a flooded inbox and panicked.

She was really, really sorry, she told me, but she simply couldn't move forward with an article.

We exchanged emails and calls. The article was back on, no it wasn't, yes it was.

You want to know what it's like to live in Monica Lewinsky's world? This is it.

I met Ms. Lewinsky the following Tuesday at her apartment.

She was rehearsing in front of a small metal music stand. Her speech coach, Pippa Bateman, was on Skype from Britain.

I quietly sat on the couch and noted the details in the room: a bookshelf blocked off the bedroom area; on it, photos of friends and family, Monica as a child. On an end table were roses, crystals and a lit candle.

She handed me a script. "It's changed a bit, so you can follow along," she said. (By the time she appeared onstage at TED, in front of a packed room, she was on Version 24 of her speech.) On the back, she had scribbled a reminder: "Push in arm muscles, engage back and neck."

She was working through the middle of the speech, where she would describe her questioning by investigators in a room not unlike the one we saw portrayed in "Slut." It was 1998, and she had been required to authenticate the phone calls recorded by her former friend Linda Tripp. They would later be released to Congress.

She glanced at the script, then looked forward.

"Scared and mortified, I listen," she said.

"Listen as I prattle on …

"Listen to my sometimes catty, sometimes churlish, sometimes silly self, being cruel, unforgiving, uncouth …

"Listen, deeply, deeply ashamed to the worst version of myself." She paused. "A self I don't even recognize."

"How did that feel?" Ms. Bateman asked. "You've got to own it."

Ms. Lewinsky doesn't have a speechwriter; she wrote the speech herself. But she has plenty of advisers: journalists, editors, new friends, old friends, her lawyer, her publicist, her family. Which is great, if everyone is in agreement. Except that no one is ever in agreement.

The major disagreement was over the opening: a joke about a man 14 years her junior, who hit on Ms. Lewinsky after she spoke at Forbes.

"What was his unsuccessful pickup line?" she would ask rhetorically. "He could make me feel 22 again. Later that night, I realized: I'm probably the only person over 40 who would not like to be 22 again."

It was funny, yes (even hysterical, judging by the reaction at TED). But did the joke sexualize her off the bat? For a woman ingrained in the public psyche as a "tart, slut, whore, bimbo," as Ms. Lewinsky put it onstage, should she try to avoid the innuendo?

Maybe she should cut that part and go straight to the next line, somebody suggested: a question for the audience.

"Can I see a show of hands," she would ask, "of anyone who didn't make a mistake or do something they regretted at 22?"

Ultimately, she stuck with the joke. (The question would stay, too.)

She performed that opening later that day in a practice session downtown, then again a few days later in front of a large gathering of friends, over wine and cheese. She would practice the speech walking down the street, running errands, on a flight from Amsterdam to Oslo. As she joked on Twitter: "If you see me walking down the streets of nyc muttering to myself, don't worry … just practicing my TED Talk."

TED approached Ms. Lewinsky about speaking at the conference, whose theme this year is "Truth and Dare," after watching her Forbes speech. Kelly Stoetzel, TED's content director, said, "Part of what I think makes this story interesting is that people will get to see all the dimensions of Monica, not just the person who was reported on 17 years ago." The idea had been marinating for years. Ms. Lewinsky often thought about the toll that shame had taken on her own life; in graduate school, she studied the impact of trauma on identity.

Then Tyler Clementi, the Rutgers freshman, killed himself after being recorded by his college roommate being intimate with a man. It was 2010, and Ms. Lewinsky's mother was beside herself, "gutted with pain," as Ms. Lewinsky said onstage, "in a way I couldn't quite understand."

Eventually, she said she realized: To her mother, Mr. Clementi represented her. "She was reliving 1998," she said, looking out over the crowd. "Reliving a time when she sat by my bed every night. Reliving a time when she made me shower with the bathroom door open."

She paused, becoming emotional. "And reliving a time both my parents feared that I would be humiliated to death."

"It was easy to forget," she said, "that 'That Woman' was dimensional, had a soul and was once unbroken."

She doesn't like to talk much about the past, but she will talk about residuals of her trauma: having to leave the movie theater every time a cop on a screen flashed a badge (a flashback to being ambushed by federal agents in the food court of the Pentagon shopping mall); the studying and reading about it, as a way to ease it.

"I had to do a lot of healing work and rehabilitation to get to what transpired over the course of the past year," she said. "Anybody who has gone through any kind of trauma knows it doesn't just go away with a snap of the fingers. It lives as an echo in your life. But over time the echo becomes softer and softer."

And yet this isn't simply about her story, she said. This was about using it to help others. As she put it, shame and humiliation have become a kind of "commodity" in our culture — with websites that thrive on it, industries created out of it, and people who get paid to clean up the mess.

What happened to compassion? she asked up on stage. "What we need," she said, "is a cultural revolution."

The way Ms. Lewinsky tells it, she was "Patient Zero" for the type of Internet shaming we now see regularly. Hers wasn't the first case ever, but it was the first of its magnitude. Which meant that, virtually overnight, she went from being a private citizen to, as she put it, "a publicly humiliated one."

"She couldn't go to a restaurant and order a bowl of soup — literally — without it being reported the next day," said Barbara Walters, who said her interview with Ms. Lewinsky was one of the most watched segments in television history.

The story was the perfect combination of politics and sex. "It was like reading a really wonderful dirty book," Ms. Walters said, "except it was her story and her mother's story and her aunt's story."

It was before the days of the Internet sex tape, but barely: Princess Diana had been photographed with a hidden camera while working out at the gym; Pamela Anderson and Tommy Lee's honeymoon sex tape was stolen from their home and bootlegged out of car trunks.

"It was at the tip of the spear of this invasive culture," said Mr. Friend, who is working on a book about the 1990s.

And so it went from there. Ms. Lewinsky was quickly cast by the media as a "little tart," as The Wall Street Journal put it. The New York Post nicknamed her the "Portly Pepperpot." She was described by Maureen Dowd in The New York Times as "ditsy" and "predatory."

And other women — self-proclaimed feminists — piled on. "My dental hygienist pointed out she had third-stage gum disease," said Erica Jong. Betty Friedan dismissed her as "some little twerp."

"It's a sexual shaming that is far more directed at women than at men," Gloria Steinem wrote me in an email, noting that in Ms. Lewinsky's case, she was also targeted by the "ultraright wing." "I'm grateful to [her]," Ms. Steinem said, "for having the courage to return to the public eye."

Had the Lewinsky story unfolded today, certainly the digital reality of it would have been worse (or at least more pungent). "They would have dug up her private photos," said Danielle Citron, a law professor and the author of "Hate Crimes in Cyberspace." But there would have also been avenues to push back: more outlets, more varied voices, probably even a #IStandWithMonica hashtag.

"If it happened today, I think the consensus that she deserved to be thrown under the bus would be considerably weaker," said Clay Shirky, a journalism professor at N.Y.U. who studies Internet culture. "And the key thing that's changed is not information — there were credible press reports about Cosby for years, just as Clinton's denial was ridiculous on its face — but the ability to coordinate reaction."

In that respect, Ms. Lewinsky may finally be in a unique position to tell her story. "I don't know ... exactly how you combat cyberbullying," Ms. Walters said. "But at least she's fighting back. ... I do think it's about time we gave her a chance."

The night before TED, Ms. Lewinsky began a ritual. She lit candles. She set up a table of crystals. She debated which necklace to wear, then ordered dinner and tea.

She would be in bed by 9:30 and up at 5 a.m.; Amy Cuddy, the Harvard researcher whose TED talk on body language clocked nearly 25 million views, was meeting her in the morning. They would power-pose together.

Ms. Lewinsky had a friend from Los Angeles there with her, and Ms. Cuddy stopped by to wish her luck. The two had never met in person.

"If you had told me a year ago I was going to be delivering a TED talk, I would have laughed in your face," Ms. Lewinsky said, seated on the carpet.

She looked at her friend.

"A year ago. ..." she choked up. "Well, you were there. It was so, so hard. There were times I thought I wouldn't make it."

"I'm just so grateful," she said. "I'm at once grateful and surprised."

Earlier, I had asked Ms. Lewinsky what she hoped to accomplish with a platform like TED. She asked if I had read the David Foster Wallace book "Brief Interviews With Hideous Men." In it, there is a chapter about suffering, and the story of a girl who has survived abuse.

What the young woman endures is horrific, said Ms. Lewinsky, but by going through it, she learns something about herself: that she can survive.

"That's part of what I thought I could contribute," she said. "That in someone else's darkest moment, lodged in their subconscious might be the knowledge that there was someone else who was, at one point in time, the most humiliated person in the world. And that she survived it."

Monica Lewinsky Breaks Her Public Silence With a TED Talk

BY JESSICA BENNETT | MARCH 19, 2015

VANCOUVER, BRITISH COLUMBIA — "You're looking at a woman who was publicly silent for a decade."

Monica Lewinsky was standing on the stage here at TED, glowing red lights behind her, a small metal music stand she had brought from home in front of her. She was in black slacks and a navy button-down. She was confident and poised. She looked like herself, only ... different.

"At the age of 22, I fell in love with my boss," Ms. Lewinsky said, looking out over the crowd of close to 1,400. "And at the age of 24, I learned the devastating consequences."

You remember Ms. Lewinsky, of course. She was the 22-year-old who had saved the dress, who was betrayed by her friend, who was threatened with jail time, and who, ultimately, became a public laughingstock.

For the last 10 years, she has mostly avoided the spotlight (though, of course, she was never out of the headlines). I have shadowed her over the last month as she — carefully — returned to the public life, culminating in her taking the stage at TED on Thursday, her most public appearance to date.

Her talk was called "The Price of Shame," and it was a call to end cyberbullying.

It was also perhaps the best way to describe Ms. Lewinsky's experience.

"Like me, at 22, a few of you may also have taken wrong turns by falling in love with the wrong person," she said to the crowd (there was a "pin-drop silence," as one attendee described it to me). "Maybe even your boss. Unlike me, though, your boss probably wasn't the President of the United States of America."

What that meant for Ms. Lewinsky, she went on to describe, was that practically overnight, she went from being a "a completely private figure to a publicly humiliated one."

She was on the cover of every newspaper. The butt of every late-night joke. She was branded "a tramp, tart, slut, whore, bimbo, and, of course, That Woman," she said. And her story was the first of its magnitude to break online, leaked to the website the Drudge Report, when Newsweek delayed its publication.

Today, said Ms. Lewinsky, that reality of the Internet magnification of humiliation is even more common. We are living, she said, in a place where humiliation has become a "commodity."

"There is a very personal price to public humiliation," she said. "And the growth of the Internet has jacked up that price."

Her talk came at the right moment. Ashley Judd has just declared she plans to press charges against the Twitter users who have harassed and threatened her, and legislators are now calling for the F.B.I. to crack down on online harassment.

The talk also follows a "This American Life" report by the writer Lindy West about meeting one of her online harassers in person. The journalist Amanda Hess recently won a National Magazine Award for her article about facing online harassment, and The Washington Post recently published an article proclaiming that the online abuse of women has become so intense that it is actually driving some female bloggers off the Internet.

"There's absolutely a cultural moment happening right now," said Ms. West, who is writing about TED for The Guardian. (She tweeted after the talk: "Dooooodz @MonicaLewinsky just killed her TED talk on online harassment so hard she got a standing ovation IN THE LOBBY.") "People are starting to understand that so much of what we refer to euphemistically — in an almost cutesy way — as 'trolling' is actually straight-ahead stalking, abuse and hate speech."

There were the expected nasty comments on Twitter. But the majority of the reaction online and in the crowd was positive.

Chris Sacca, the venture capitalist, called it "one of the best, most courageous TED talks ever."

Shonda Rhimes, the creator of "Scandal," simply tweeted: "YES."

"She's incredibly brave," said the Harvard researcher Amy Cuddy (whose own TED Talk on the power pose has clocked 25 million hits), adding that she was "very glad she had this opportunity."

Ms. Lewinsky hopes the conversation won't end there. "What we need," she said, preparing to wrap up, "is a cultural revolution ... It's time for an intervention on the Internet and in our culture."

Shortly before she walked off the stage, she said, "You can insist on a different ending to your story."

The Ornithologist the Internet Called a Murderer

OPINION | BY KIRK WALLACE JOHNSON | JUNE 15, 2018

FOR SOME TIME, I'd been searching for Christopher Filardi, a biologist with decades of field experience in the Solomon Islands. I wanted to interview him for a book I was writing, but the email system at the American Museum of Natural History, which once listed him as the director of Pacific programs at its Center for Biodiversity and Conservation, bounced back my message.

The auto-reply said that he'd moved to another organization, Conservation International. When I wrote him there, another auto-reply informed me that he had moved on. I couldn't find him on Facebook or Twitter. The man seemed to have vanished.

When I finally found a working number for him, he was reluctant to talk. Three years ago, his life was overturned by an online mob that accused him of murder. The fact that the mob's outrage was driven by ignorance didn't make it any less frightening.

A 2017 Pew study reported that 40 percent of Americans have experienced some form of online harassment, but what Dr. Filardi experienced was far worse than a few mean tweets. He has never given an interview about what happened. He agreed to tell his story on the condition that I not reveal where he lives.

In September 2015, Dr. Filardi and a team of researchers from the museum and the University of the South Pacific ascended the rugged Chupukama Ridge, on Guadalcanal, one of the Solomon Islands, which he described in his field journal as "a sky island filled with scientific mystery." The goal of the mission was not only to study Guadalcanal's ecosystems, but to make the case for preserving them at a time when the Solomon Islands are under pressure to open more land up to logging and mining.

On the third morning, the sound of "kokoko-kiew" pulsed through the forest. The call was unmistakably a forest kingfisher's. Dr. Filardi's heart raced. For 20 years, he'd been searching for the mustached kingfisher, known as a "ghost" bird. Only three individuals, all female, had been discovered by scientists over the past century. There were no male specimens in any of the world's museums; not even a photo of one was known to exist. He got a glimpse of the bird, just a flash of blue and gold, before it vanished.

Days later, when the team captured a male in a mist net, Dr. Filardi gasped. "One of the most poorly known birds in the world was there, in front of me, like a creature of myth come to life," he wrote in a dispatch to the museum.

While the expedition was still underway, the museum released the first photographs of the bird, which seemed to be mugging for the camera. The mustached kingfisher became a viral celebrity, under headlines like "ridiculously gorgeous."

It wasn't until the public realized that Dr. Filardi had "collected" the bird — killing it for the museum's research collection — that the adulation turned to venom.

Marc Bekoff, a researcher focusing on animal consciousness at the University of Colorado, Boulder, fumed on HuffPost that killing " 'in the name of education' or 'in the name of whatever' simply needs to stop." He added, "It is wrong and sets a horrific precedent for future research and for children."

Colleen O'Brien, a director at PETA, condemned it as "perverse, cruel and the sort of act that has led to the extinction of other animals who were also viewed as 'specimens.' " All that was needed to document the bird, she argued, was "compassion, awe and a camera, not disregard and a death warrant."

While Dr. Filardi was still on the mountain, almost entirely off the grid, the rage spread. Tens of thousands of people signed petitions that condemned his actions, and thousands more signed a petition calling for him to be fired, or even jailed.

PING ZHU

The museum frantically tried to reach him. People were trying to hack into his Facebook account, which was quickly disabled. The pages of his children were targeted. His wife began receiving phone calls with death threats, at all hours of the night. A petition that stated, "Chris Filardi is a disgrace and frankly does not deserve to breathe another breath," was signed by 3,798 people.

He descended from the mountaintop into an inferno of hate. "If they wanted to make me feel horrible and more than a little frightened for my family or welfare," he told me, his voice strained, "it worked."

When he returned to the museum in New York, police officers told him to "be conscious" of how he entered it, never walking in the front door with the rest of the public, but using a back door instead.

Dr. Filardi hoped the threats were just talk, but he kept thinking back to May 2001, when an eco-terrorist group known as the Earth Liberation Front firebombed the Center for Urban Horticulture at the University of Washington, where Dr. Filardi was a graduate student.

The bombing was aimed at the work of a professor they mistakenly believed was releasing genetically engineered poplar trees into the wild. (No one was hurt.)

Still, Dr. Filardi wanted to engage, if only to defend his field and the museum, which he had been visiting since his childhood. "I felt like a failed ambassador of the natural sciences," he told me.

He wrote an essay for Audubon explaining the many steps he'd taken to ensure that the taking of a single kingfisher would not cause harm, including a survey of the population, which he estimated at 4,000 — a "robust number for a large island bird." He highlighted the role the bird played in conservation efforts: After his findings were presented to tribal, local and national officials, they resolved to protect the area from being mined or logged.

His essay received over 900 comments, the most up-voted of which called him a murderer.

The mustached kingfisher was not gathered for public display, as a "trophy," as many claimed. It resides in a carefully maintained part of the museum dedicated to research alongside nearly a million other ornithological specimens, none of which spawned death threats.

Some of the birds in the world's museum and university collections were gathered before the word "scientist" was even coined. The naturalist Alfred Russel Wallace described them as the "individual letters" that "make up one of the volumes of our earth's history." Each scientific advance — the discovery of the nucleus, viruses, genes, DNA — has led to new ways of studying the same historic birds.

These collections have also directly contributed to policies that have helped wildlife. The pesticide DDT was ultimately banned after a comparison of museum egg specimens revealed that shells had grown thinner after it was introduced. A study of 120 years' worth of seabird skins demonstrated rising levels of mercury in the ocean.

The collections almost certainly hold answers to questions that researchers haven't yet thought to pose about the changes happening to our planet. And in this age of the Sixth Extinction, the collections are becoming even more vital.

When I asked Dr. Filardi whether he could have obtained what he needed for research by simply plucking a feather — a suggestion made by many online — he bristled. "All a feather gets you is DNA, and that's not a magic wand!" With the specimen, though, "we have RNA, a skeleton, gonads, tissues in cryogenic storage."

He continued, "In 100 years, there's going to be all sorts of ways to utilize this that we don't even know yet."

This is not just his opinion, but the overwhelming consensus among field biologists. After a 2014 article in Science suggested that specimen collection might play a role in species extinction unless a code of ethics was adopted, over 100 museum and university researchers signed a strident rebuttal, outlining the rigorous legal and ethical guidelines already governing collecting.

Those condemning a scientist for killing one bird might first wrestle with the fact that American house cats kill as many as four billion backyard birds a year. An additional 600 million to 900 million birds slam into our buildings. The mining of rare metals used to build the very phones and computers that Dr. Filardi's detractors used to call for his head endanger the survival of birds and other creatures those people claim to defend.

It's also no coincidence that the uproar seems reserved for only the most beautiful animals. The same month that Dr. Filardi's life was upended, a team led by Jake Esselstyn of Louisiana State University discovered a new species, the hog-nosed rat, on the Indonesian island of Sulawesi. The rat, which has uniquely long pubic hair, was killed and preserved for future research, but there are no petitions calling for Dr. Esselstyn's firing.

In the end, it was Dr. Filardi's children — who had grown up in the age of cyberbullying — who reassured him that the online threats were unlikely to translate into real-world violence. They helped him understand what he described as "the nameless ease with which people can violently assault and denigrate, to feed a sense of righteousness" before moving on to their next digital target.

Although Facebook and Twitter have outlined the types of threats — murder, sexual assault and breaking bones — that violate their rules, the burden is usually on those being threatened to flag the comments. Moderators are overwhelmed, and punishments are often as mild as a "time out." Artificial intelligence isn't a magical fix, either: Last fall, a Japanese Twitter user's account was frozen after what was probably an algorithm flagged him for tweeting a death threat at a mosquito.

Nine months after he discovered the mustached kingfisher, Dr. Filardi left the American Museum of Natural History. He told me that he was worried about doing damage to an institution that he loved — people were threatening to pull donations — but that he was not pushed out. He still collaborates with the museum and with Conservation International, and has just returned to the Solomon Islands with a new organization.

Before he left for the islands, he told me he was "not bitter" about what had happened.

"I understand and empathize with the challenge of confronting the taking of another life to feed the intellect of humans," he said. "I try to give people the benefit of the doubt."

But I couldn't help but be outraged on his behalf that people claiming to act in wildlife's name had ruthlessly harassed someone who had done more than most of us to understand and protect the natural world. And I worried about the effect of that harassment on other scientists in his field.

Van Remsen, the curator of birds at Louisiana State University's Museum of Natural Science, told me that the Filardi affair hasn't changed his mind about the importance of collecting. "Almost every kingfisher that has ever lived has suffered a more painful death than the one Filardi collected, either being eaten alive by a predator or from the inside by a disease," he said. "If we thought for a second that what we were doing is wrong in terms of hurting populations, we wouldn't be doing it."

But it has led him — and many other ornithologists with whom I spoke, almost all of whom asked me not to use their names — to be extremely cautious about attracting any kind of attention. Many research expeditions are no longer being publicized; in some cases, there is a total blackout on media. As a result, the public will grow even less informed about the importance of this research.

You can't blame the scientists. One distinguished ornithologist lamented the new culture of fear. "Some crazy vegan lady just shot up YouTube," he said. "Who knows what could happen?"

KIRK WALLACE JOHNSON is the author of "The Feather Thief: Beauty, Obsession, and the Natural History Heist of the Century."

The Rise of the Internet Fan Bully

BY AMANDA HESS | AUG. 12, 2016

NORMANI KORDEI, a member of the girl group on the rise Fifth Harmony, sat for a lighthearted Facebook Live interview earlier this month. Within a week, she had been chased off Twitter by a mob spewing racist insults.

"I've not just been cyber bullied, I've been racially cyber bullied with tweets and pictures so horrific and racially charged that I can't subject myself any longer to the hate," she wrote. Her account has been silent since.

Online harassment has become a depressingly common workplace hazard for people of color in the public eye. Last month, the "Ghostbusters" star Leslie Jones temporarily quit Twitter after weathering a deluge of racist abuse. And last year, the Brazilian actress Taís Araújo reported a series of harassers to the police after they had inundated her Facebook page with similar comments.

But the racist taunts hurled at Ms. Kordei didn't originate from some white supremacist message board, or even from a crew of Fifth Harmony haters. It came from within the Fifth Harmony fandom itself.

The incident illuminates some strange similarities between the bands of internet trolls stalking the web and the legions of online fans seeking to stir up some drama. They both know that the most hurtful weaponry to wield against black women include images of apes, threats of lynching and a tossed-off N-word.

Fifth Harmony is a Simon Cowell-assembled girl group that snagged its first Top 10 hit this year with the saucy single "Work From Home." Its brand would best be described as "gyrating girl power." But when Ms. Kordei sat down with the digital lifestyle magazine Galore for the Facebook Live interview on the subject of female friendship, one question — "Describe each girl in one word" — ripped a fault line through the group's young, female fan base.

Of her bandmate Ally Brooke, Ms. Kordei said: "Sunshine, because she is literally the light of the group." Of Lauren Jauregui: "My therapist, I can go to her about absolutely anything, and I feel like I can trust that she won't judge anything that I say." And Dinah Jane: "She's like the turn-up queen, she just has a good time anywhere she is." When she reached Fifth Harmony's final member, Camila Cabello, she paused. "She is ... let's see. Camila. Very quirky. Yeah, very quirky. Um, cute. Quirky."

That's it. But that was enough to enrage some fans of Ms. Cabello, the 19-year-old who has been positioned as Fifth Harmony's breakout star (and earned a spot in Taylor Swift's squad). To this set, Ms. Kordei's answer was apparently insufficiently effusive. "Camila is a lot more than cute and quirky she's kind, classy, mature and hardworking," one fan tweeted.

The backlash soon grew big enough to hit the teen gossip sites ("OMG: Did Normani Kordei Throw Shade at Camila Cabello?" the magazine J-14 asked), before curdling into something more sinister. In fan enclaves across the web, a subset of Fifth Harmony followers called Ms. Kordei "Normonkey," "coon," and "nigger." One said she "deserves to be lynched." Another Photoshopped her face onto the body of a woman hanging from a tree.

This is the kind of rhetoric you expect to see on 4chan's political message board, a den of white supremacist rhetoric fused with ironic memes. The trolls of 4chan have lately helped power the online presence of the alt-right, the folks who led the Twitter assault against Ms. Jones. Now the internet's most unruly celebrity fans are cribbing their troublemaking tactics from the same playbook.

The firestorm against Ms. Jones was touched off by a nasty review of "Ghostbusters" published by Milo Yiannopoulos, a conservative provocateur. As the attacks built, comment threads unspooled inside 4chan, surfacing racist images and commentary to hurl at Ms. Jones in Twitter's open marketplace. Abuse against Ms. Kordei was organized, too, by an anonymous Twitter account that popped up directing fans to inundate her with slurs.

KARSTEN MORAN FOR THE NEW YORK TIMES

Zayn Malik received slurs like "terrorist" when he was with the British boy band One Direction.

Trolls thrive off provoking a response from their targets. When Ms. Jones began speaking out against the abuse on Twitter, 4chan posters traded gleeful messages. Fans, too, delight in forging some connection with the stars, even if it comes in the form of a rebuke. The abuse against Ms. Kordei escalated after she took to Twitter to deny a feud with Ms. Cabello and to denounce the fans attempting to stir up trouble. That behavior eventually scored a response from Ms. Cabello, too. "You don't have to hate on somebody else to support me — I don't appreciate it and it's not what I'm about," she tweeted. "Be kind or move on."

Most Fifth Harmony fans, who call themselves Harmonizers, are not racists. As the abuse mounted, support for Ms. Kordei poured out under the hashtags #IStandWithNormani and #WeLoveYouNormani. Still, racially tinged remarks about Ms. Kordei have been a low-level presence amid her rise in popularity — fans have expressed surprise that she reads books and called her "ugly" and "ape" — and the abuse tends to flare at dramatic moments within the roiling fan narrative of imagined alliances and feuds (like the supposed ongoing beef between Ms. Kordei and Ms. Cabello).

A similar dynamic has played out among One Direction fans, some of whom have greeted Zayn Malik, the group's lone Muslim member, with death threats and slurs like "terrorist." He briefly quit Twitter in 2012, citing Islamophobia, and left the band last year. And when Robert Pattinson started dating the singer FKA Twigs in 2014, a subgroup of his fans inundated her with racist abuse on Twitter that left her "genuinely shocked and disgusted."

Some level of infighting is embedded within pop fandom itself. Like One Direction before it, Fifth Harmony is a Cowell-engineered pop group that's been perfectly primed to exploit differences in personality, style and ethnic background of the group's singers. The Spice Girls played this trick most baldly, naming and dressing members after a singular trait — Baby, Scary, Sporty, Posh and Ginger. But supporting a favorite bandmate can easily degrade into trashing a least favorite. In a New York Post article from 1998, one 9-year-old Spice Girls fan said of Ginger (Geri Halliwell): "A lot of people don't like her. I think some people hate her the most out of all of them." She added: "I personally don't like Scary Spice, though."

Typically, girl group loyalism falls into the benign end of human self-sorting. But in the crucible of online fandom, demographic distinctions can coarsen into warring factions. A fan fantasy that frames the band members as hating one another — and paints one of them as rude, stupid, evil, and deserving of death because she is black — is no longer just idle fan fictions. As Ms. Kordei put it in one of her notes to fans, "For those of you who enjoy speculating creating drama that doesn't exist, please keep in mind that myself and the other girls in the group are PEOPLE."

She added: "This is our story so let us write it our way, instead of you trying to write it for us."

CHAPTER 3

Technology Evolves

The problem of cyberbullying will not be solved without changes in the way technology is used. The rise and fall of anonymous sharing apps such as Yik Yak and Secret, explored in this chapter, may indicate a positive pattern. And the creative application of artificial intelligence in detecting harassment on social media could point toward a kinder and more productive online future.

Can Bots Fight Bullying?

BY ANNA NORTH | SEPT. 21, 2016

IF A TEENAGER gets bullied on social media, it's usually up to her to report the incident. But one day, an automated tool might spot the harassment, ask her if she needs help, tell a moderator to step in on her behalf or notify her parents.

While rudimentary filters for bad language have existed for years, tech companies and others are experimenting with tools that use machine learning, crunching through huge numbers of online interactions to "train" themselves to identify bullying.

The Google subsidiary Jigsaw has developed a tool called Conversation AI, which uses machine learning to identify harassment. Jigsaw trained the tool with the help of institutions, including The New York Times, which provided 17 million reader comments from The Times's website along with decisions that moderators had made about whether to accept or reject them. Analyzing comments that moderators had flagged as abusive helped Conversation AI improve.

Mary Aiken, a cyber security expert, proposes a similar approach in her new book "The Cyber Effect." She hopes to create a database of user-submitted examples of harassment that can be used to develop an anti-bullying tool.

A number of other researchers and companies, including SRI International, which created Siri, have explored machine-learning responses to online harassment in recent years.

These efforts have the potential to change the way social networks and other technology and media companies handle harassment. Bullying is difficult to identify in part because the same phrase can be insulting in one context and affectionate in another, said Norman Winarsky, the former president of SRI's ventures group. But by analyzing millions or billions of conversations, new tools could begin to identify patterns that distinguish innocent comments from harassment.

The technology isn't foolproof. When Andy Greenberg at Wired tested Conversation AI with a real example of harassment directed at another writer, the tool rated the obvious threat as fairly benign.

While AI tools are likely to improve over time, humans will probably always need to monitor them for accuracy and make the final decision in difficult cases. Companies that use the tools will have to ensure that their users consent to having their interactions monitored by a computer program. Identifying harassment, of course, is only the first step to protecting users of social networks. Just as important is how quickly the companies respond to acts of harassment once their tools spot that behavior.

A Founder of Secret, the Anonymous Social App, Is Shutting It Down

BY MIKE ISAAC | APRIL 29, 2015

LAST SUMMER, employees at the start-up Secret gathered in their new offices in downtown San Francisco, waiting for the founders to address the company. Secret had recently raised $25 million to work on its smartphone app, which lets users anonymously share information with groups of friends and connections.

But the news had broken that David Byttow and Chrys Bader, the founders of Secret, had sold part of their stake in the company for $6 million and that Mr. Byttow later bought a Ferrari. The founders did not initially tell the employees about the sale; instead, some of them found out on Secret.

Although Mr. Byttow and Mr. Bader reassured workers at the meeting that they were dedicated to the company, it was a turning point, said people close to Secret, who spoke on condition of anonymity. It shook the confidence of some workers, they said: If the founders had taken money off the table, it could mean they were protecting themselves against Secret's failing.

On Tuesday, that course of events played out. After use of the app declined for months, Mr. Byttow told employees that the company was closing and handed out severance packages, the people close to the matter said.

"After a lot of thought and consultation with our board, I've decided to shut down Secret," Mr. Byttow wrote in an online post on Wednesday shortly after BuzzFeed reported that the start-up would close. He said he would wind down Secret over the next few weeks and would return money to investors. "I believe in failing fast in order to go on and make only new and different mistakes."

Secret's trajectory illustrates the flash-in-the-pan nature of Silicon Valley's current technology boom. Even as a handful of start-ups rise to stratospheric valuations and take in billions of dollars in financing, other privately held companies cannot sustain their following.

Fab.com, a onetime e-commerce darling, was once valued at more than $1 billion and had raised more than $150 million before ending up in a fire sale this year, when it was bought for about $15 million. Other start-ups are dealing with a cooling-off process as big companies muscle in on their turf. Meerkat, a live-streaming video app that gained great traction early this year, is now grappling with the entrance of Twitter and its Periscope live-video app, for example.

Yet even by Silicon Valley standards, Secret's arc from next big thing to yesterday's news was breathtakingly fast. The app was started 16 months ago by Mr. Byttow and Mr. Bader, one of a group of anonymous-sharing apps that includes Whisper and Yik Yak. Mr. Byttow had previously worked at Google building social networking products, and at other hot start-ups, such as the mobile payments company Square.

Within weeks, Silicon Valley was abuzz about Secret. The venture capitalist Marc Andreessen sent several Twitter messages at the time that appeared to attack the gossip and rumors circulating on apps like Secret. At the same time, other investors were rushing to buy into Secret. In March 2014, the company raised $8.6 million from venture capital firms such as Kleiner, Perkins, Caufield & Byers and celebrities including Ashton Kutcher.

Part of the reason the app had momentum was that it focused on issues of anonymity and identity, themes that many in Silicon Valley imagined would be part of the next wave of social networking apps after Facebook and Twitter.

Alexis Ohanian, a founder of Reddit who invested in Secret, said at the time that it showed signs of being a contender for the future of social networking beyond Facebook. "Apps like Secret become an outlet for people to speak honestly about things that would otherwise result in career damage," Mr. Ohanian said. He did not respond to a request for comment on Wednesday.

"They raised a lot of money and had a good reaction initially," said Brian Blau an analyst at Gartner, a research company. "But how do you build viral growth when the community is anonymous?"

Mr. Byttow tried to stoke enthusiasm for Secret. In a post last March, he wrote that 75 percent of users with more than five friends came back every day. "Our vision is to create a world flowing with authenticity," he wrote. "Being more open with each other brings us closer together, builds understanding and ultimately makes the world a better place."

Interest was so great that Secret's co-founders had private discussions with Chris Cox, vice president of product at Facebook, about anonymity and identity, according to two people with knowledge of the meeting. Facebook declined to comment.

Still, Secret was controversial. For many, it was a morass of vitriol and catty comments, a playground for anonymous cyberbullies to take potshots at others. Secret scrambled to hire community moderators to control the negative posts. People inside Secret said it was not prepared to deal with the flood of negative posts.

More money flowed in. Secret raised $25 million from Index Ventures, Redpoint Ventures and others in July, giving it a valuation of more than $100 million.

To broaden the app's appeal, the start-up released a new version that would let people sign up for Secret and find friends using their Facebook credentials, instead of using the contacts in someone's address book. The company added other features, including an ability to more easily browse topics in the app.

Even so, use appeared to decline, according to App Annie, an analytics firm. Last August, a Brazilian court ordered Apple and Google to remove the app from their app stores in the country over concerns that it promoted cyberbullying.

Many close watchers of Secret have seen the writing on the wall for some time. In the last six months, nearly all of Secret's top engineering employees have gone to other companies, including Uber, Airbnb and Twitter.

In December, Secret redesigned its app to look much like Yik Yak, a competitor, in hopes of attracting more users. It did not work, and use declined further, two people with knowledge of the figures said. Subsequently, Mr. Bader left Secret over differences about what it should become.

Closing Secret "has been the hardest decision of my life and one that saddens me deeply," Mr. Byttow wrote on Wednesday. "Unfortunately, Secret does not represent the vision I had when starting the company, so I believe it's the right decision for myself, our investors and our team."

Mr. Byttow's once-prized red Ferrari is also gone, a person with knowledge of the matter said.

Secret's Doomed Script

OPINION | BY JOE NOCERA | MAY 5, 2015

IN EVERY EPISODE of "Silicon Valley," the terrific HBO comedy series created by Mike Judge, there is always a moment, rendered utterly deadpan, that both mocks and explains the current, are-we-in-a-bubble-yet state of play in, well, Silicon Valley.

In one episode this season, for instance, the show's hero, Richard Hendricks, the nerdy founder of Pied Piper, mentions the plans he has "once we have a subscription-revenue model." His backer, an obnoxious billionaire, leaps out of his seat. "No, no, no!" he exclaims. "Why would you go after revenue?"

"To make money?" Richard answers meekly. "If you have no revenue, you can say you are prerevenue," explains the billionaire. "You're a potential pure play. It's not about how much you earn; it's about what you're worth. And who's worth the most? Companies that lose money!"

In other episodes this season, we've been introduced to an app called "Bro" — its only function is to allow someone to send the word "bro" to someone else — and the coming of "datageddon," thanks to all the "selfies and useless files people refuse to delete."

And, of course, there is the way all the young, scruffy entrepreneurs on "Silicon Valley" profess to be in business to "make the world a better place" rather than to get rich. "We're making the world a better place through Paxos algorithms for consensus protocols," says one company founder at a TechCrunch Disrupt conference.

"And we're making the world a better place through software-defying data centers for cloud computing," says another.

Which perhaps explains why I immediately thought of Judge's parody of life in techland as I read the real-life news last week that the social app Secret was shutting down after only 16 months. Like many of the fake companies on "Silicon Valley," Secret was based on a truly ridiculous idea: that an app that allowed people to send anonymous messages would not only be a hit, but would "reduce the barrier to communication" and make it possible to convey the "raw truth" without that annoying filter of identity. Anonymity was going to be the next big thing in "social," according to its founders, David Byttow, 33, and Chrys Bader-Wechseler, 31.

"It helps you become a better person if you want to be a better person," Byttow told the audience at — where else? — a TechCrunch Disrupt conference.

Internet anonymity can make you a better person? Since when? Hadn't we learned long ago that cyberbullying, gossip of the rankest sort, and the spreading of false rumors were the usual results of web anonymity, crowding out other, more ennobling responses.

But Byttow — who only wears black in public, to judge by his various YouTube appearances — and Bader-Wechseler were convinced that making it easy for people to post anonymous messages (to their friends, no less) would, indeed, make the world a better place. Or at least they convinced enough gullible venture capitalists of this that they were able to raise some $35 million during their company's short life, reaching a valuation at one point of $100 million.

As for revenue, it pretty much followed the "Silicon Valley" model. Any interviewer who asked how a completely anonymous "community" could serve as the foundation for a money-making business was told, quite matter of factly, that it was far too early to contemplate such mundane matters. Searching for a revenue model "would be a distraction at this point," Byttow explained to the technology journalist Kara Swisher, who occasionally plays her sardonic, all-knowing self on "Silicon Valley." "You have to build liquidity in your users," added Bader-Wechseler.

So what happened to Secret? Cyberbullying was a problem from the start, which seemed to surprise the founders, who were in a constant struggle to keep control of the posts. Security and privacy were also issues. ("We have learned a lot!" Bader-Wechseler told an interviewer five months in.) Brazil ordered it shut down. Marc Andreessen criticized it. As the app's novelty wore off, people stopped using it. Byttow and Bader-Wechseler responded by redesigning the site so that it more closely resembled Yik Yak, a more successful competitor.

Employees started leaving, including Bader-Wechseler in January. Meanwhile, as The Times reported, the founders had each taken $3 million off the table in the second round of financing, and Byttow had bought a red Ferrari (which, The Times also reported, he has since gotten rid of). Most new tech companies that realize their business model is doomed spend the rest of their money by "pivoting" to something more promising. Byttow instead decided to return the leftover money to his investors. A classy touch.

In the blog post in which he announced that he was shutting down the Secret app, Byttow promised that he would "publish postmortems so that others can learn from the unique mistakes and challenges we faced and the wisdom gained from such an incredible 16 months."

No doubt Mike Judge will be taking notes for future episodes.

JOE NOCERA is an Op-Ed columnist for The New York Times.

Who Spewed That Abuse? Anonymous Yik Yak App Isn't Telling

BY JONATHAN MAHLER | MARCH 8, 2015

DURING A BRIEF RECESS in an honors course at Eastern Michigan University last fall, a teaching assistant approached the class's three female professors. "I think you need to see this," she said, tapping the icon of a furry yak on her iPhone.

The app opened, and the assistant began scrolling through the feed. While the professors had been lecturing about post-apocalyptic culture, some of the 230 or so freshmen in the auditorium had been having a separate conversation about them on a social media site called Yik Yak. There were dozens of posts, most demeaning, many using crude, sexually explicit language and imagery.

After class, one of the professors, Margaret Crouch, sent off a flurry of emails — with screenshots of some of the worst messages attached — to various university officials, urging them to take some sort of action. "I have been defamed, my reputation besmirched. I have been sexually harassed and verbally abused," she wrote to her union representative. "I am about ready to hire a lawyer."

In the end, nothing much came of Ms. Crouch's efforts, for a simple reason: Yik Yak is anonymous. There was no way for the school to know who was responsible for the posts.

Eastern Michigan is one of a number of universities whose campuses have been roiled by offensive "yaks." Since the app was introduced a little more than a year ago, it has been used to issue threats of mass violence on more than a dozen college campuses, including the University of North Carolina, Michigan State University and Penn State. Racist, homophobic and misogynist "yaks" have generated controversy at many more, among them Clemson, Emory, Colgate and the University of Texas. At Kenyon College, a "yakker" proposed a gang rape at the school's women's center.

IAN THOMAS JANSEN-LONNQUIST FOR THE NEW YORK TIMES

Jordan Seman, a junior at Middlebury College in Vermont, came across a Yik Yak post last year that made a sexual reference to her and compared her to a "hippo."

In much the same way that Facebook swept through the dorm rooms of America's college students a decade ago, Yik Yak is now taking their smartphones by storm. Its enormous popularity on campuses has made it the most frequently downloaded anonymous social app in Apple's App Store, easily surpassing competitors like Whisper and Secret. At times, it has been one of the store's 10 most downloaded apps.

Like Facebook or Twitter, Yik Yak is a social media network, only without user profiles. It does not sort messages according to friends or followers but by geographic location or, in many cases, by university. Only posts within a 1.5-mile radius appear, making Yik Yak well suited to college campuses. Think of it as a virtual community bulletin board — or maybe a virtual bathroom wall at the student union. It has become the go-to social feed for college students across the country to commiserate about finals, to find a party or to crack a joke about a rival school.

Much of the chatter is harmless. Some of it is not.

"Yik Yak is the Wild West of anonymous social apps," said Danielle Keats Citron, a law professor at University of Maryland and the author of "Hate Crimes in Cyberspace." "It is being increasingly used by young people in a really intimidating and destructive way."

Colleges are largely powerless to deal with the havoc Yik Yak is wreaking. The app's privacy policy prevents schools from identifying users without a subpoena, court order or search warrant, or an emergency request from a law-enforcement official with a compelling claim of imminent harm. Schools can block access to Yik Yak on their Wi-Fi networks, but banning a popular social media network is controversial in its own right, arguably tantamount to curtailing freedom of speech. And as a practical matter, it doesn't work anyway. Students can still use the app on their phones with their cell service.

JOSHUA LOTT FOR THE NEW YORK TIMES

"I have been defamed, my reputation besmirched. I have been sexually harassed and verbally abused. I am about ready to hire a lawyer," said Margaret Crouch, professor of philosophy at Eastern Michigan University, after learning of comments posted about her on Yik Yak.

Yik Yak was created in late 2013 by Tyler Droll and Brooks Buffington, fraternity brothers who had recently graduated from Furman University in South Carolina. Mr. Droll majored in information technology and Mr. Buffington in accounting. Both 24, they came up with the idea after realizing that there were only a handful of popular Twitter accounts at Furman, almost all belonging to prominent students, like athletes. With Yik Yak, they say, they hoped to create a more democratic social media network, one where users didn't need a large number of followers or friends to have their posts read widely.

"We thought, 'Why can't we level the playing field and connect everyone?' " said Mr. Droll, who withdrew from medical school a week before classes started to focus on the app.

"When we made this app, we really made it for the disenfranchised," Mr. Buffington added.

Just as Mark Zuckerberg and his roommates introduced Facebook at Harvard, Mr. Buffington and Mr. Droll rolled out their app at their alma mater, relying on fraternity brothers and other friends to get the word out.

Within a matter of months, Yik Yak was in use at 40 or so colleges in the South. Then came spring break. Some early adopters shared the app with college students from all over the country at gathering places like Daytona Beach and Panama City. "And we just exploded," Mr. Buffington said.

Mr. Droll and Mr. Buffington started Yik Yak with a loan from Mr. Droll's parents. (His parents also came up with the company's name, which was inspired by the 1958 song, "Yakety Yak.") In November, Yik Yak closed a $62 million round of financing led by one of Silicon Valley's biggest venture capital firms, Sequoia Capital, valuing the company at hundreds of millions of dollars.

The Yik Yak app is free. Like many tech start-ups, the company, based in Atlanta, doesn't generate any revenue. Attracting advertisers could pose a challenge, given the nature of some of the app's content.

For now, though, Mr. Droll and Mr. Buffington are focused on extending Yik Yak's reach by expanding overseas and moving beyond the college market, much as Facebook did.

Yik Yak's popularity among college students is part of a broader reaction against more traditional social media sites like Facebook, which can encourage public posturing at the expense of honesty and authenticity.

"Share your thoughts with people around you while keeping your privacy," Yik Yak's home page says. It is an attractive concept to a generation of smartphone users who grew up in an era of social media — and are thus inclined to share — but who have also been warned repeatedly about the permanence of their digital footprint.

In a sense, Yik Yak is a descendant of JuicyCampus, an anonymous online college message board that enjoyed a brief period of popularity several years ago. Matt Ivester, who founded JuicyCampus in 2007 and shut it in 2009 after it became a hotbed of gossip and cruelty, is skeptical of the claim that Yik Yak does much more than allow college students to say whatever they want, publicly and with impunity. "You can pretend that it is serving an important role on college campuses, but you can't pretend that it's not upsetting a lot of people and doing a lot of damage," he said. "When I started JuicyCampus, cyberbullying wasn't even a word in our vernacular. But these guys should know better."

Yik Yak's founders say the app's overnight success left them unprepared for some of the problems that have arisen since its introduction. In response to complaints, they have made some changes to their product, for instance, adding filters to prevent full names from being posted. Certain keywords, like "Jewish," or "bomb," prompt this message: "Pump the brakes, this yak may contain threatening language. Now it's probably nothing and you're probably an awesome person but just know that Yik Yak and law enforcement take threats seriously. So you tell us, is this yak cool to post?"

In cases involving threats of mass violence, Yik Yak has cooperated with authorities. Most recently, in November, local police traced the source of a yak — "I'm gonna [gun emoji] the school at 12:15 p.m. today" — to a dorm room at Michigan State University. The author, Matthew Mullen, a freshman, was arrested within two hours and pleaded guilty to making a false report or terrorist threat. He was spared jail time but sentenced to two years' probation and ordered to pay $800 to cover costs connected to the investigation.

In the absence of a specific, actionable threat, though, Yik Yak zealously protects the identities of its users. The responsibility lies with the app's various communities to police themselves by "upvoting" or "downvoting" posts. If a yak receives a score of negative 5, it is removed. "Really, what it comes down to is that we try to empower the communities as much as we can," Mr. Droll said.

When Yik Yak appeared, it quickly spread across high schools and middle schools, too, where the problems were even more rampant. After a rash of complaints last winter at a number of schools in Chicago, Mr. Droll and Mr. Buffington disabled the app throughout the city. They say they have since built virtual fences — or "geo-fences" — around about 90 percent of the nation's high schools and middle schools. Unlike barring Yik Yak from a Wi-Fi network, which has proved ineffective in limiting its use, these fences actually make it impossible to open the app on school grounds. Mr. Droll and Mr. Buffington also changed Yik Yak's age rating in the App Store from 12 and over to 17 and over.

Toward the end of last school year, almost every student at Phillips Exeter Academy in New Hampshire had the app on his or her phone and checked it constantly to read the anonymous attacks on fellow students, faculty members and deans.

"Please stop using Yik Yak immediately," Arthur Cosgrove, the dean of residential life, wrote in an email to the student body. "Remove it from your phones. It is doing us no good."

At Exeter's request, the company built a geo-fence around the school, but it covered only a few buildings. Students continued using the app on different parts of the sprawling campus.

"We made the app for college kids, but we quickly realized it was getting into the hands of high schoolers, and high schoolers were not mature enough to use it," Mr. Droll said.

The widespread abuse of Yik Yak on college campuses, though, suggests that the distinction may be artificial. Last spring, Jordan Seman, then a sophomore at Middlebury College, was scrolling through Yik Yak in the dining hall when she happened across a post comparing her to a "hippo" and making a sexual reference about her. "It's so easy for anyone in any emotional state to post something, whether that person is drunk or depressed or wants to get revenge on someone," she said. "And then there are no consequences."

In this sense, the problem with Yik Yak is a familiar one. Anyone who has browsed the comments of an Internet post is familiar with the sorts of intolerant, impulsive language that the cover of anonymity tends to invite. But Yik Yak's particular design can produce especially harmful consequences.

TRAVIS DOVE FOR THE NEW YORK TIMES

The Yik Yak mascot outside a fraternity at the University of North Carolina at Chapel Hill last week. The anonymous digital bulletin board has been a hit, if a problematic one, at colleges across the country.

"It's a problem with the Internet culture in general, but when you add this hyper-local dimension to it, it takes on a more disturbing dimension," says Elias Aboujaoude, a Stanford psychiatrist and the author of "Virtually You." "You don't know where the aggression is coming from, but you know it's very close to you."

Jim Goetz, a partner at Sequoia Capital who recently joined Yik Yak's board, said the app's history of misuse was a concern when his firm considered investing in the company. But he said he was confident that Mr. Droll and Mr. Buffington were committed to ensuring more positive interactions on Yik Yak, and that over time, the constructive voices would overwhelm the destructive ones.

"It's certainly a challenge to the company," Mr. Goetz said. "It's not going to go away in a couple of months."

Ms. Seman wrote about her experience being harassed on Yik Yak in the school newspaper, The Middlebury Campus, prompting a schoolwide debate over what to do about the app. Unable to reach a consensus, the paper's editorial board wrote two editorials, one urging a ban, the other arguing that the problem wasn't Yik Yak but the larger issue of cyberbullying. (Middlebury has not taken any action.)

Similar debates have played out at other schools. At Clemson, a group of African-American students unsuccessfully lobbied the university to ban Yik Yak when some racially offensive posts appeared after a campus march to protest the grand jury decision's not to indict a white police officer in the fatal shooting of an unarmed black teenager in Ferguson, Mo. "We think that in the educational community, First Amendment rights are very important," said Leon Wiles, the school's chief diversity officer. "It's just problematic because you have young people who use it with no sense of responsibility."

During the fall, Maxwell Zoberman, the sophomore representative to the student government at Emory, started noticing a growing number of yaks singling out various ethnic groups for abuse. "Fave game to play while driving around Emory: not hit an Asian with a truck," read one.

"Guys stop with all this hate. Let's just be thankful we arn't black," read another.

After consulting the university's code, Mr. Zoberman discovered that statements deemed derogatory to any particular group of people were not protected by the school's open expression policy, and were in fact in violation of its discriminatory harassment rules. Just because the statements were made on an anonymous social-media site should not, in his mind, prevent Emory from acting to enforce its own policies. "It didn't seem right that the school took one approach to hate speech in a physical medium and another one in a digital medium," he said.

Mr. Zoberman drafted a resolution to have Yik Yak disabled on the school's Wi-Fi network. He recognized that this would not stop students from using the app, but he nevertheless felt it was important for the school to take a stand.

After Mr. Zoberman formally proposed his resolution to the student government, someone promptly posted about it on Yik Yak. "The reaction was swift and harsh," he said. "I seem to have redirected all of the fury of the anonymous forum. Yik Yak was just dominated with hateful and other aggressive posts specifically about me." One compared him to Hitler.

A few colleges have taken the almost purely symbolic step of barring Yik Yak from their servers. John Brown University, a Christian college in Arkansas, did so after its Yik Yak feed was overrun with racist commentary during a march connected to the school's World Awareness Week. Administrators at Utica College in upstate New York blocked the app in December in response to a growing number of sexually graphic posts aimed at the school's transgender community.

In December, a group of 50 professors at Colgate University — which had experienced a rash of racist comments on the app earlier in the fall — tried a different approach, flooding the app with positive posts.

Generally speaking, though, the options are limited. A student who felt that he or she had been the target of an attack on Yik Yak could theoretically pursue defamation charges and subpoena the company to find out who had written the post. But it is a difficult situation to imagine, given the cost and murky legal issues involved. Schools will probably just stand back and hope that respect and civility prevail, that their communities really will learn to police themselves.

Yik Yak's founders say their start-up is just experiencing some growing pains. "It's definitely still a learning process for us," Mr. Buffington said, "and we're definitely still learning how to make the community more constructive."

Spying on College Life, via Yik Yak

BY LORI ROZSA | JAN. 11, 2015

I'M A RECOVERING HELICOPTER PARENT with an only child who is now in college. The transition for her has been wonderful, almost seamless. For me, not so much.

I've tried to show some self-restraint. I tapered off my obsessive checking of her phone-tracking app after the first week or so. I resisted the urge to call or text her first. I curtailed my gratuitous offering of advice on everything from laundry to class selection. I let her go.

And I was pretty miserable as a result. I missed having her at home, but there was also a less noble reason — after 18 years of knowing who her friends were, befriending her friends' parents, getting to know her teachers and school and curriculum, and knowing a good bit about the rest of her life as well, I was out of the loop. As any involved parent will tell you, that is a painful place to be.

Then I discovered Yik Yak. Now I feel better.

I know I'm not supposed to. Yik Yak is a free app that lets anonymous users write on a scrolling feed that is geofenced, allowing only people within a limited range (say, a college campus) to post. Any time social media is blended with anonymity, trouble and ugliness are inevitable. And so it is with Yik Yak. At barely a year old the app has not only become popular on college campuses, but has also been roundly condemned by many parents, educators and others. Some campuses have moved to ban it. Eric Stoller, writing in Inside Higher Ed, called it "a drug-fueled rave filled with miscreants." "Fairly disgusting," he concluded.

It can be. It's aimed at a college audience, and it's written mostly by college students, so there is a lot of talk about sex, drugs and unpleasant bodily functions. But if you skip the nasty posts (which can be "downvoted" and consequently dropped from the site pretty quickly), it can also be amusing — there are a lot of young Jimmy Fallons and Amy Poehlers out there — and very informative.

Yik Yak has a feature called "Peek" that allows anybody to take a look at what college students across the country and elsewhere are thinking and talking about. If you happen to have a kid at one of those colleges, you can get some insight into what is going on there, the good and the bad. That's why I peek. It's like an unofficial newsfeed from a college, targeting just that campus. It's not what you see on Facebook and Twitter, and it is definitely not the view you get at Parents and Family Weekend.

If you had looked on the University of Virginia's yak scroll recently, for example, you would have seen the debate about sexual assault and the news media played out in real time among some of the people most affected by it. Same thing if you had happened to be looking at Florida State University's Yik Yak during the campus shooting there in November. You would have found fear, and also offers of comfort and support among students on a traumatized campus.

But most of the time, it's just the musings and commentary of college students who seem to relish the sense of community, even if they are anonymous. They talk about the campus buses and the dining hall food, they announce pizza specials or give tips when the line at Starbucks is short, or when they got a free side of guacamole at Chipotle.

A few consistent themes emerge after just a few days peeking at Yik Yak, no matter what campus you tune in to: Students complain (a lot) about the lack of sleep, the lack of money, poor quality toilet paper on campus, inconsiderate roommates and the weather.

And they may not tell their parents, but they really miss a lot about home, including, in this order of popularity: their dogs, home cooking, their own beds, their cats, mom and dad.

College rivalries are a constant as well: "Forgot to shower, accidentally got a degree in Hippie Studies from Brown," read a Yak from Cornell University in September.

Relationship issues, loneliness and other personal, yet anonymous details, are another popular theme such a this post from the Davidson College-area Yik Yak in December: "Nothing more ironic than hiding your gay pride flag in your closet so your parents don't see it when they come to pick you up."

As a parent, I find some value in those shared experiences and the glimpse into the lives of some of my daughter's classmates, no matter how banal or, occasionally, how disquieting they may be.

A group of Colgate University professors recently flooded their college's Yik Yak with positive messages to counteract cyberbullying — and students liked it. The professors said they probably won't continue to "yak." But I bet that, like me, they will continue to peek.

In Rise of Yik Yak App, Protests and Ethics Collide

BY WILLIAM D. COHAN | APRIL 7, 2015

DO VENTURE CAPITALISTS and other highly sophisticated and compensated investors, like those controlling large private equity and hedge funds, have any moral or ethical responsibility for the investments they make?

Should the smart-money crowd be held accountable for the harm caused to people who use the products and services created with the money that springs from their coffers?

Or is the bottom line the only thing that matters when it comes to investing?

These questions come to mind when considering the turmoil caused on college campuses nationwide by Yik Yak, the anonymous messaging service founded in 2013 by Tyler Droll and Brooks Buffington soon after they graduated from Furman University in Greenville, S.C. Not surprisingly, the immense popularity of Yik Yak has attracted the attention of venture capitalists looking for the next Facebook.

Within months of starting its service — with a loan from Mr. Droll's parents — Yik Yak began collecting venture capital money. The first round of financing was a modest $1.5 million from a group of small venture capitalists in and around the company's Atlanta headquarters. Two months later, Yik Yak raised an additional $10 million from many of the original investors, as well as a V.C. heavyweight, Tim Draper, the founder of Draper Fisher Jurvetson. Then, last November, Yik Yak hit the jackpot when Sequoia Capital, the granddaddy of all Silicon Valley venture capitalists, led a $62 million round of equity financing that valued the company at $200 million to $300 million.

Yik Yak allows localized groups of people to post instant messages anonymously for other people in the same area to see, on whatever subjects they want. Yik Yak knows the identities of its users and has constructed its privacy policies to make it nearly impossible for it to share names without a subpoena or court order. The reach of the service is limited to a 1.5-mile radius from a local service node, making Yik Yak well suited to college campuses. Think of it as Twitter without user profiles, either fictitious or genuine.

Yik Yak allows for real-time social and political commentary about events that are happening — and that seem so excruciatingly important at any given moment — on campuses across the country, but it also permits an unleashing of the basest human instincts that result, too often, in forms of cyberbullying.

"Think of it as a virtual community bulletin board — or maybe a virtual bathroom wall at the student union," Jonathan Mahler wrote in The New York Times last month. "It has become the go-to social feed for college students across the country to commiserate about finals, to find a party or to crack a joke about a rival school. Much of the chatter is harmless. Some of it is not."

And that in a nutshell is the problem. According to Mr. Mahler, Yik Yak "has been used to issue threats of mass violence on more than a dozen college campuses, including the University of North Carolina, Michigan State University and Penn State. Racist, homophobic and misogynist 'yaks' have generated controversy at many more, among them Clemson, Emory, Colgate and the University of Texas. At Kenyon College, a 'yakker' proposed a gang rape at the school's women's center."

More than 78,000 people have signed an online petition urging that Yik Yak be shut down. Just as we do not allow someone to yell "Fire!" in a crowded theater, shouldn't there be limits to hateful, anonymous speech that can unfairly tarnish a life forever or cut one short? And shouldn't the Sequoia Capitals and Tim Drapers of the world bear some responsibility for financing businesses where such behavior is not only permitted but also actively encouraged through the cover of anonymity?

To try to get some answers, I reached out to Jim Goetz, the Sequoia Capital partner responsible for the firm's investment in Yik Yak and a new member of the company's board. Mr. Goetz may be one of the most successful venture capitalists of all time; he is the man behind Sequoia's extraordinarily successful investments in YouTube, Instagram, PayPal and WhatsApp. When Facebook bought WhatsApp in 2014 for about $20 billion in Facebook stock, Sequoia made more than 50 times its $60 million investment. Needless to say, Mr. Goetz is a busy man and much in demand.

My written questions to him ranged from why Sequoia decided to make the investment to how he feels about the controversy Yik Yak has generated to ones about whether venture capitalists have any moral or ethical responsibility for the investments they make? This latter question is one that Paul Tudor Jones, the billionaire hedge fund manager and founder of the Robin Hood Foundation, tackled in a highly regarded TED Talk last month.

After voicing his concern about the growing gap between rich and poor in this country, Mr. Jones said he was creating Just Capital, a nonprofit organization dedicated to trying to make sure investors and companies do the right things, not just the expedient and profitable ones. "When we begin to put justness on par with profits, we get the most valuable thing in the world. We get back our humanity," he said.

I was hoping to have a conversation about all this with Mr. Goetz. Does he agree with Mr. Jones, for instance? But he demurred.

"This is not a list that we can address with a quick weekend call," he wrote me. Alas, he did not offer another time for a call during business hours. Instead, Mr. Goetz answered, by email, two of my questions.

As to why Sequoia made its investment, Mr. Goetz wrote, "Yik Yak has tapped our desire to connect authentically with those around us. Its hyper-local forums provide a sense of community and a place to be our genuine selves, and that's really resonated with millions of people, myself included."

As for the controversy that Yik Yak has generated on the matter of cyberbullying, Mr. Goetz wrote, "I know Yik Yak takes cyberbullying very seriously and has made a number of meaningful changes to address it, such as proactively geo-fencing middle and high school campuses so the app simply can't be used there. Cyberbullying is a broad and thorny challenge faced by all social media networks and there's clearly more work to be done, but Yik Yak is definitely moving in the right direction."

Beyond that, Mr. Goetz directed me to Hilary McQuaide, Yik Yak's new director of communications. As one would expect, her answers were filled with the usual corporate pablum. Was there anything else she could help me with, Ms. McQuaide wondered? Why yes, I answered: I would still like to hear from Mr. Goetz on the question of what responsibility venture capitalists bear, if any, for financing companies that encourage anonymous cyberbullying? I am still waiting.

WILLIAM D. COHAN is a former senior mergers and acquisitions banker who has written three books about Wall Street. His latest book is "The Price of Silence: The Duke Lacrosse Scandal, the Power of the Elite, and the Corruption of Our Great Universities."

The Rise and Fall of Yik Yak, the Anonymous Messaging App

BY VALERIYA SAFRONOVA | MAY 27, 2017

THIS MONTH, two feminist groups and several former students filed a federal complaint accusing the University of Mary Washington in Virginia and its former president, Richard Hurley, of failing to protect the female plaintiffs from cyber harassment and threats of physical and sexual violence during their time at the university.

The platform where all of this took place? Yik Yak, the now-defunct, localized, anonymous messaging app that Tyler Droll and Brooks Buffington, two students at Furman University in South Carolina, founded in 2013 and that soon became associated with bullying, discriminatory speech and threats of bomb and gun violence.

"The lack of responsiveness and inability to control this devastating hate speech I think is what ultimately did this app in," said Debra Katz, one of the lawyers who brought the complaint against Mary Washington, located in Fredericksburg, and Mr. Hurley, in federal court for the Eastern District of Virginia.

In response to the suit, the university said it contained "no new allegations" and that it had, and would continue, to "work diligently to create a safe and secure campus environment and to address the issue of sexual violence."

There was no comment from Mr. Hurley's lawyer.

The lawsuit was just the latest twist in the rocky road the messaging app has traveled in its short life.

In March 2014, a school in Massachusetts evacuated its students twice after Yik-Yak-based bomb threats, and during the same month, a high school in California was put on lockdown for a similar reason.

In October 2014, Jordan Seman, a student at Middlebury College in Vermont, posted an open letter about being targeted on the app for her weight. "I felt exposed, betrayed and mostly embarrassed," she wrote.

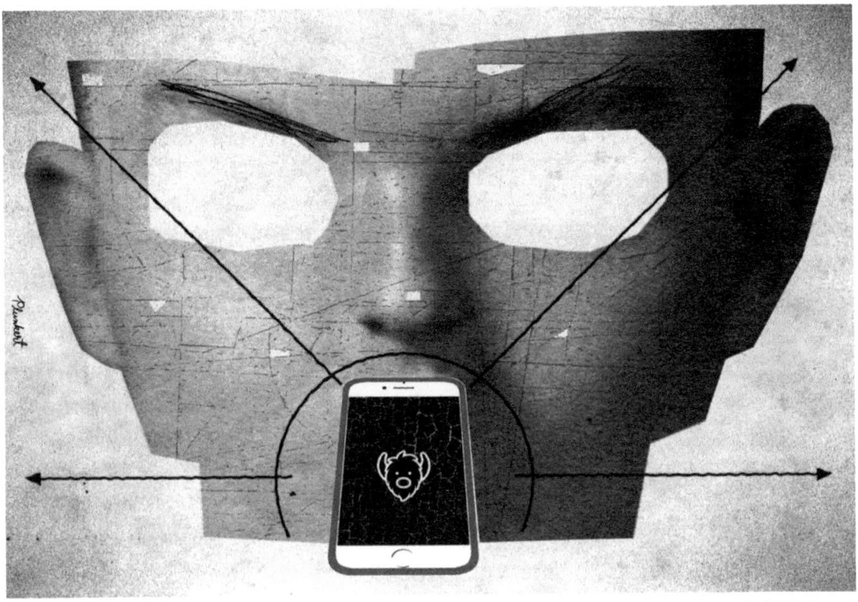

DAVID PLUNKERT

The next month, two other high schools in California were put on lockdown after threats of violence, and in Michigan, the police arrested Matthew Mullen, a student at Michigan State whose Yik Yak post threatened a shooting. Mr. Mullen was eventually sentenced to two years' probation and ordered to pay $800 in restitution for the investigation.

At the University of Missouri, campus police arrested Hunter M. Park and charged him with making threats of violence against black students on Yik Yak. Mr. Park received a three-year suspended sentence and five years' probation after pleading guilty to making a terrorist threat. A former Virginia Tech student pleaded guilty to using the app to threaten a repeat of the 2007 campus shooting in which 32 people were killed.

The high point for Yik Yak came in 2014, when its founders raised $73 million in venture-capital funding. According to App Annie, a firm that tracks metrics for apps, downloads spiked in September of that year and stayed high for several months. But by early 2015, the decline began. App Annie estimates that Yik Yak had 1.8 million downloads in September 2014. By September 2016, it was 125,000.

At the end of that year, Mr. Droll and Mr. Buffington laid off 60 percent of their employees, and last month, they shut down the operation, selling off intellectual property and employee contracts to Square Inc., a mobile payment company, for $1 million. A few months earlier, Hive, a college-based chat app with a similar color scheme to Yik Yak's, popped up in the iTunes and Google Play stores, with Mr. Buffington in one of the screenshots. Whether it was an attempt at reinvention under the Yik Yak umbrella or a side project is unclear, but it is no longer available.

Yik Yak's image problems seemed to stem from its reliance on anonymous posts and the few solutions that were available to curtail racist, sexist, aggressive or threatening language. The app was community-monitored, meaning that users could vote down a post they found vulgar or offensive, and if the post received enough negative feedback, it was removed.

RAYMOND MCCREA JONES FOR THE NEW YORK TIMES

Tyler Droll, left, and Brooks Buffington created Yik Yak while college students in 2013. Once enormously popular and lucrative, it traveled a rocky road to oblivion.

But the app's privacy policy did not allow institutions to identify users who posed a risk without a subpoena, court order or search warrant, or an emergency request from a law-enforcement official with a compelling claim of imminent harm.

Though neither Yik Yak nor its creators were named as defendants in the suit against Mary Washington and Mr. Hurley, the app's role was central. Its name is mentioned 51 times in the 35-page complaint, which outlines instances when members of the campus group Feminists United were targeted in "Yaks," or messages on the platform, after they spoke out against Greek life on campus and were connected with the suspension of a rugby team, some of whose members had sung a song "that called for violence against women, including rape and necrophilia" at a party, according to the complaint.

Messages that cropped on Yik Yak disparaged and threatened the feminist group's most visible members. Some of the worst are listed in the complaint: "Gonna tie these feminists to the radiator and [g]rape them in the mouth," "Can we euthanize whoever caused this?"

Kelli Musick, one of the plaintiffs, who graduated in 2015, said: "There were days when I felt like I couldn't look away from my phone because a friend or someone I knew would send me a screenshot of a threatening or harassing Yak. We don't blame the app in and of itself. It was a tool. Tools can be used in any way that a person decides to use them."

But the group did ask the university to request that Yik Yak place a virtual fence around its campus to disable the app. The solution was one Yik Yak had begun using in March 2014 in Chicago-area schools and one it gradually expanded to middle and high schools nationwide after facing criticism from parents and educators.

"We had parents reaching out to say their 9-year-old has been threatened and harassed on the app," said Ross Ellis, the founder and chief executive of Stomp Out Bullying. "Kids get hysterical when people make mean comments. Their brains are not mature enough to handle it."

The school administration, citing logistical and First Amendment concerns, refused. So the group asked that Yik Yak be banned on the school's Wi-Fi network, a gesture that was primarily symbolic given that students could continue to access it on their personal data plans. The university said no again.

"This was something over which we had no control," said Anna Billingsley, the associate vice president for university relations. "We couldn't remove the posts from Yik Yak." She said that the school offered the protection of campus police and suggested that the students contact Yik Yak and the Title IX office at the university.

"They told us to report the Yaks to Yik Yak, and if they were found to be credible, Yik Yak would then respond, which is not the case for any other threats of violence on campus," Ms. Musick said. "When it has been a threat of a bomb or a gun, other schools did not say, 'Report it to Yik Yak and they'll follow up.' "

In trying to react to complaints about its product, Yik Yak created geo-fences and added filters that recognized certain keywords, such as "bomb," and would ask users if they wanted to proceed with the message by suggesting: "Pump the brakes, this Yak may contain threatening language. Now it's probably nothing and you're probably an awesome person but just know that Yik Yak and law enforcement take threats seriously. So you tell us, is this Yak cool to post?"

But little changed and students at schools across the country began to fight back. The College of Idaho student senate requested that Yik Yak geo-fence their campus, and in Georgia Emory University's student government denounced the app in a formal resolution. Students at Clemson University in South Carolina unsuccessfully demanded that the school ban the app after a spate of racist messages.

And at the University of Mary Washington, Ms. Musick and her classmates turned to Ms. Katz to file a complaint with the Education Department. Its Office of Civil Rights opened an investigation, but before it could issue a decision, the White House changed hands and many of the office's employees left. So the women went to district court.

Yik Yak tried to put in place further preventive measures in 2016 first by allowing users to have profiles and handles, then by requiring them. After blowback, the identity markers became optional once again.

Despite these efforts, by this past March, about two and a half years after it had closed a round of funding that raised millions in venture capital, its active users over age 18 had fallen to 264,000, an enormous decline from nearly 1.9 million in November 2014, according to comScore.

Was Yik Yak really that bad? A study at the MIT Media Lab that compared it to Twitter found that posts on the anonymous platform were only slightly more likely to contain vulgar words. The difference was less than 1 percent. "We find that on anonymous platforms, users are only slightly more likely to use vulgar language than on public ones, and when they do it is not acceptable and leads to negative feedback," the authors wrote.

Morgan Hines, who will start her fourth year at Northeastern University in Boston this fall, never encountered nastiness on Yik Yak. "I thought it was funny," she said. "It formed a lot of camaraderie between students. There would be random shout-outs to things happening on campus, like people who are attractive or being annoying in the library, or a fire alarm going off at 4 a.m."

But Ms. Hines criticized Yik Yak's hyper-localization. "Yik Yak was for pockets of people on campus," she said. "If the fire alarm went off at 4 a.m., it only went off at your building, so no one else will give it a thumbs-up."

That hyper-localization is also what made the cases of harassment particularly galling. Ms. Musick, one of the plaintiffs, said, "With Yik Yak, in the back of your mind, you know they're not from around the world or other parts of the state, they're right there in your classroom, in your dining hall. On a campus with 4,500 students, that's a pretty small group of people. This isn't some creepy guy in his mom's basement in Indiana."

In the end, it may have been this aspect of the app that really did it in. Danielle Levitas, the senior vice president for research at App Annie, pointed out that bad press would not necessarily override an app's popularity if it fulfilled a useful function (consider Uber, for example). But, she said, if it does not have something sustainable to offer, it will burn out.

In this case, it seems that being local was to Yik Yak's detriment. When Ms. Hines went home to Kentucky after her freshman year, she forgot about the app. "I wasn't on campus anymore and I wasn't with my friends anymore," she said. And back at Northeastern, "no one was on campus to comment on anything." She added, "It kind of just became irrelevant in my life."

Name-Calling in the Virtual Playground

BY NICK BILTON | MARCH 23, 2014

SILICON VALLEY sometimes feels like high school. It has its alpha types and its outcasts, its bullies and its bullied.

That, anyway, is one takeaway from the recent flap over Secret, a six-week-old social app that connects people anonymously. Secret has apparently put the Valley in touch with its inner 10th grader and become a cyber-schoolyard for all manner of gossips and trolls inside the technology industry. The blowback has been swift.

Veronica Belmont, a video host and technology writer, promptly hung up on the app. "Deleted the app Secret," Ms. Belmont wrote in early February.

Aaron Durand, a photographer, soon followed. "It's not me, it's you," Mr. Durand tweeted a few days later. Many others followed suit.

"I don't need that kind of hate in my life," one entrepreneur told me. "It's like high school all over again."

If this is what happens in the temples of American technology, think what will happen when Secret and similar apps hit real high schools and middle schools. Parents, you have been warned.

The founders of Secret, Chrys Bader-Wechseler and David Byttow, told me that they saw the potential pitfalls and were trying to find ways to prevent cyberbullying over their app before it finds its way to youngsters. They said Secret was supposed to help people, not hurt them.

And yet the dangers of these types of apps are clear. Cyberbullying is bad enough when you know who is doing the bullying. It can be even worse when the source is cloaked by design. Last year, nine teen suicides were linked to bullying on Ask.fm, a website that lets people ask questions and leave comments anonymously.

The issue became so severe that Ask.fm hired Mishcon de Reya, a law firm based in London, to conduct an independent review of the site. That, in turn, prompted Ask.fm, which is based in Latvia, to create tools that give users the ability to turn off questions from anonymous users, block unwanted users and report offensive content.

Ilja Terebin, chief executive of Ask.fm, said that the company was aware of the challenges but that young people needed places to express their views privately.

"On one hand, we have to deliver a value for our users, which includes free speech and uninhibited communication," Mr. Terebin said. "On the other hand, we must ensure that the most vulnerable groups of our users receive sound support and protection."

But how can we offer people — adults and teens alike — anonymity without encouraging bad behavior? A lot of experiments are underway. A new social app called Facefeed lets people share photos, but only allows people to discuss the photos in a private message. Shots, a social app for selfies, has forgone a comment system altogether. "With comments, kids can be humiliated in front of a large audience," said John Shahidi, a founder of Shots.

Yik Yak, which is similar to Secret and lets people post anonymously to their friends, said last week that it was banning middle and high school students and that it would disable the service around schools.

Yik Yak has reportedly been used to taunt students and make bomb threats, raising concern among school authorities. Susan Opferman, the principal of Webb Bridge Middle School in Alpharetta., Ga., recently warned parents in a letter: "Yik Yak posts can be especially vicious and hurtful, since there is no way to trace their source."

To reduce negative comments, Secret has said that it is adding features that detect when people's names are typed into in messages and warn those who would include them to "think before they post." Users also have the ability to ban those who trash-talk others.

"The majority of the content on the app is positive and friendly," said Mr. Bader-Wechseler, Secret's chief product and design lead. "We have to be realistic. We're living in a world that is not a utopia, and we need to make sure we're taking all the right steps to make sure that the good outweighs the evil." For now, Mr. Bader-Wechseler said, the company is learning what not to do when the app does fall into the hands of children. But it's unclear if the app has already been infused with the DNA of bullies and those bullied. And, if so, if it's possible to change that.

I asked Mr. Terebin at Ask.fm if he had any advice for Secret and other anonymous apps. He said these services should build moderating systems and empower users to report bad behavior.

"This means that companies must invest in their safety protocols from the very beginning," Mr. Terebin said.

An App Combats Bullying, One Anonymous Compliment at a Time

BY STACY SUAYA | DEC. 20, 2016

Name Austin Kevitch
Age 25
Hometown Blue Bell, Pa.

Now Lives In a 3,500-square-foot Craftsman house in Santa Monica, Calif., that he shares with four employees and his younger sister.

Claim to Fame Mr. Kevitch is the founder of Brighten, an app that allows users to send compliments to friends anonymously, as a kind of antidote to social media bullying. "It feels good to make someone smile," reads the app's tagline. Mr. Kevitch said that more than 10 million messages have been sent by its one million users, many of whom are in high school and college.

Big Break The idea for Brighten came to Mr. Kevitch in 2013, when he was a junior at Bucknell University. A close friend, Oliver, died in a climbing accident, and his Facebook page was filled with positive remembrances. "I wished Oliver could've read those messages while he was still alive," Mr. Kevitch said. He built the app, which he envisioned as a digital compliment box, with a programmer he met through the Kairos Society, an organization that brings young entrepreneurs together to solve the world's problems. "I paid a couple thousand dollars; it was my life savings at the time," Mr. Kevitch said. The app was released in 2014, and drew 5,000 users in its first three months.

Latest Project Mr. Kevitch just returned from Summit at the Sea (think Ted Talks meets Coachella on a cruise ship), where he shared ideas on entrepreneurship and wellness with the likes of Will.i.am and Wim Hof, the Dutch daredevil nicknamed "The Iceman."

NATHANIEL WOOD FOR THE NEW YORK TIMES

A friend's death served as the impetus for Austin Kevitch's anti-bullying app.

"Wim was my favorite," Mr. Kevitch said. "He thinks he has the cure for depression." That cure? Take 25 deep breaths.

Next Thing Brighten is looking to team up with anti-bullying platforms including Kind Campaign, a nonprofit group that combats what it calls "girl on girl" bullying, and Be Cool Be Nice, a social media campaign started by Willow Smith and Kendall Jenner built around the hashtag #BeCoolBeNice and the idea that "Kindness is always in style."

Humble Start Mr. Kevitch's first brush with a compliment box came during high school, when he was a guest at a friend's house. His little sister set down a compliment box, made from an old tissue box. "Write something nice about a family member," she said. A few minutes later, she pulled out pieces of paper and read all the compliments. "It brightened everyone's day," Mr. Kevitch said.

Found on Facebook: Empathy

BY TEDDY WAYNE | OCT. 9, 2015

IN A WIDELY CIRCULATED CLIP from "Conan" in 2013, Louis C. K. went into a jeremiad against cellphones. Among other criticisms, he argued that they were destroying the ability of children to feel for others.

"They don't look at people when they talk to them and they don't build empathy," he said. "Kids are mean, and it's 'cause they're trying it out. They look at a kid and they go, 'You're fat,' and then they see the kid's face scrunch up and they go, 'Ooh, that doesn't feel good to make a person do that.' "

"But when they write, 'You're fat,' " he continued, pantomiming typing on a phone, "then they just go, 'Mmm, that was fun, I like that.' "

The riff was a darkly humorous version of what has become conventional wisdom about the increasing number of screens and our decreasing capacity for empathy.

Sherry Turkle's new book, "Reclaiming Conversation," and a pile of research and many highly publicized cases of cyberbullying have backed up this assertion, especially as it pertains to youth.

A 2010 study from the University of Michigan found that the empathy of college students between 1979 and 2009 dropped off considerably after 2000, with the researchers speculating that the rising prominence of personal technology was one of several factors.

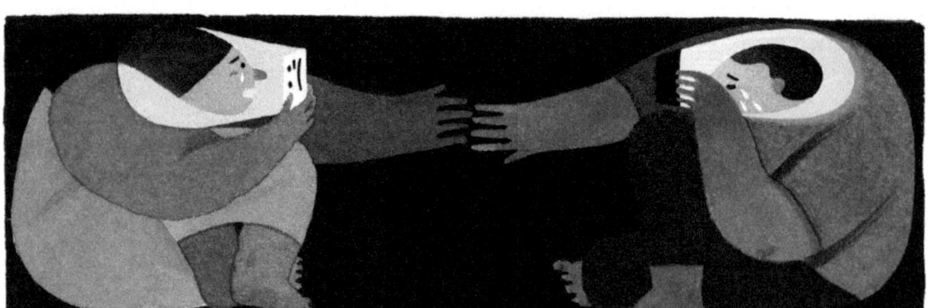

ELEANOR DAVIS

Yet there is a different interpretation of young people's levels of empathy, one that takes into account their far greater tolerance today for lifestyles and values not their own. Larry D. Rosen, a psychology professor at California State University, Dominguez Hills, who specializes in the effects of technology, worked on a recent study in the journal Computers in Human Behavior that measured the impact of spending time online on real-world empathy.

Dr. Rosen's team found that being on the Internet "does not displace face-to-face time nor reduce real-world empathy" and that "virtual empathy was positively correlated with real-world empathy."

Empathy, their study suggests, can be dispensed and felt virtually, though in-person empathy — a hug, for instance, as opposed to a Facebook "like" — has six times the impact on feelings of social support. (The study also found that the specific type of online activity can be crucial; playing video games, for example, had "negative effects" on empathy.)

"I don't think it's a problem with a lack of empathy, but a different style," Dr. Rosen said in an interview. "We have to think of empathy as a continuum. The experience that we hear from kids and young adults is they do feel like they're being empathetic."

This new style of empathy may play out most saliently in acceptance of people whom previous generations have judged more harshly. According to the General Social Survey, administered by the research organization NORC at the University of Chicago, the percentage of American adults who viewed homosexuality as "always wrong" rose through the 1970s and '80s, peaking in AIDS-phobic 1987 at three-quarters of the population.

As of 2014, the most recent year for which data are available, it stands at 40 percent, overshadowed by the 49 percent who think there is nothing wrong with homosexuality, while support for same-sex marriage, especially among 18-to-34-year-olds, has risen sharply.

Dr. Rosen credits at least some of this considerable change to social media.

"Now we're all so open and seemingly somewhat honest behind the screen," he said, "so there's more opportunity to observe it and go, 'Hey, this friend of a friend is going through a gender-change operation, and I see it on his Facebook page.' We have more of an opportunity to build up a feeling of fairness and equality because we're exposed to much more of everybody's lives now."

While critics of social media may contend that seeing someone's status update is a weak replacement for a person-to-person conversation, "that indirect access feels to younger people like direct access," Dr. Rosen said. "It's substituted for it. They feel more connected rather than less connected."

A 2014 study from the University of North Florida found patterns suggesting "that Facebook, in facilitating great social connection, may encourage some aspects of empathy in contrast to previous reports."

One reason we may condemn social media for its narcissism is because we view it as a monolith, when there are numerous subcategories of its use. There is a great difference, for instance, between posting a dozen selfies at a rooftop party versus linking to a charity's donation page and writing a personal statement about the cause.

The study, which drew mostly from unmarried participants, examined how empathy changed related to a few user activities on Facebook, including private chat and messages and publicly commenting on status updates.

Men scored higher than females on "Perspective Taking" — that is, a cognitive "ability to place oneself in another's situation" — from both private messages and public commenting, although those actions were negatively correlated with "Personal Distress," or "the anguish felt during others' hardships and troubles."

Women were not affected as much by these two activities, though the researchers noted that they "scored significantly higher than males in all empathy subscales, except for Perspective Taking."

What these findings suggest is that certain types of Facebook interaction may help a person put himself in another's shoes — and, in this study at least, it is usually a "himself" who gains the most benefit, even if it doesn't always result in the Clintonian registration of pain.

"In face-to-face connections, you tend to stay with people you're most familiar with or have most in common with," said Tracy Alloway, an associate professor of psychology and the lead author of the paper. "But Facebook can break down those boundaries. We can be exposed to different ways of thinking and emotional situations. On a somewhat superficial level, individuals disclose things about themselves, and that facilitates maybe not a deep sense of closeness, but the next time you see them, you may feel you know them a little better."

Well, she might. A Pew Research Center report from January found that women with an average-size Facebook network are aware of 13 percent more stressful events in the lives of their friends than those without an account; for men, it was an 8 percent increase. Not only was women's awareness of these events higher than men's, but their increased awareness leads them to bear a greater "cost of caring" than men (though researchers also noted that "women report higher levels of stress to begin with").

Moreover, the younger the user, the more aware he or she was of these stressful events, a finding that suggests the youngest generation may be the most amenable to screen-based opportunities for empathy.

The major progressive shift of attitudes about homosexuality in recent decades certainly has more to do with political changes and activism than it does with the Internet. And social media, as any tentative tiptoe through YouTube comments or Twitter posts reveals, is still often a pit of hatred, intolerance and bullying.

But it has gotten better. While the tormentor in Louis C. K.'s scenario may be lacking compassion, perhaps there will be others who see his meanspirited message and, instead of piling on, feel for the victim.

Instagram Unveils a Bully Filter

BY LAURA M. HOLSON | MAY 1, 2018

INSTAGRAM SAID TUESDAY it was expanding its online anti-bullying initiative, adding a new filter to weed out comments meant to harass or bully the 800 million users of the popular social media site.

The company said it would review accounts that have a large number of comments filtered out. If those accounts violate Instagram's community guidelines, it will take action, which could include banning them. The new filter will also hide comments attacking a person's appearance or character, and alert Instagram to repeat offenders.

It is the second step in an initiative announced last year to curb offensive comments and rid Instagram of its most malicious members.

"To be clear, we don't tolerate bullying on Instagram," Kevin Systrom, the company's chief executive and co-founder, told Instagram users in a blog post Tuesday. The company will also expand policies to guard against the bullying of young public figures who are often the target of hate-filled messages.

"Protecting our youngest community members is crucial to helping them feel comfortable to express who they are and what they care about," he added.

In a 2017 study conducted by Ditch the Label, an online anti-bullying organization, 71 percent of respondents in the United Kingdom said social media sites did not do enough to combat online bullying. Instagram was of particular note: 42 percent of more than 10,000 people aged 12 to 20 surveyed in the United Kingdom said they had experienced cyberbullying on the site in the previous 12 months.

In March, the model and actress Amber Rose called out cyberbullies for saying her 5-year-old son was gay after she posted videos on Instagram of him opening a gift from the singer Taylor Swift.

It is not only children who are targeted. In November, Drew Barrymore was attacked after she posed with a starfish in a photograph to promote a new lipstick. "It hurt me," she wrote in a follow-up post, which was liked 484,238 times.

Instagram, like other social media sites including Twitter and YouTube, has become an easy place to shame or offend, something the company acknowledged last year. Mr. Systrom addressed it in a blog post then, saying, "Many of you have told us that toxic comments discourage you from enjoying Instagram and expressing yourself freely."

Instagram is using a machine-learning algorithm to detect offenders. Called DeepText, it was built by Facebook, which owns Instagram, and uses artificial intelligence to review words for context and meaning, much as the human brain determines how words are used. (Facebook is holding its annual F8 developer conference this week.) Initially, Instagram had a team of people review and rate comments, sorting them into different categories: bullying, racism or sexual harassment.

"What we are concentrating on is building the tools so people can control their experience on Instagram," said Karina Newton, head for public policy at Instagram. "Those will improve over time."

Instagram's users are expected to follow the site's guidelines, which include being respectful to other community members and not posting photographs of naked bodies.

The company has also embarked on a "kindness" campaign, hosting events to promote inclusion and diversity. "It's been our goal to make it a safe place for self expression and to foster kindness within the community," Mr. Systrom said. "This update is just the next step in our mission to deliver on that promise."

Girl's Suicide Points to Rise in Apps Used by Cyberbullies

BY LIZETTE ALVAREZ | SEPT. 13, 2013

MIAMI — The clues were buried in her bedroom. Before leaving for school on Monday morning, Rebecca Ann Sedwick had hidden her schoolbooks under a pile of clothes and left her cellphone behind, a rare lapse for a 12-year-old girl.

Inside her phone's virtual world, she had changed her user name on Kik Messenger, a cellphone application, to "That Dead Girl" and delivered a message to two friends, saying goodbye forever. Then she climbed a platform at an abandoned cement plant near her home in the Central Florida city of Lakeland and leaped to the ground, the Polk County sheriff said.

In jumping, Rebecca became one of the youngest members of a growing list of children and teenagers apparently driven to suicide, at least in part, after being maligned, threatened and taunted online, mostly through a new collection of texting and photo-sharing cellphone applications. Her suicide raises new questions about the proliferation and popularity of these applications and Web sites among children and the ability of parents to keep up with their children's online relationships.

For more than a year, Rebecca, pretty and smart, was cyberbullied by a coterie of 15 middle-school children who urged her to kill herself, her mother said. The Polk County sheriff's office is investigating the role of cyberbullying in the suicide and considering filing charges against the middle-school students who apparently barraged Rebecca with hostile text messages. Florida passed a law this year making it easier to bring felony charges in online bullying cases.

Rebecca was "absolutely terrorized on social media," Sheriff Grady Judd of Polk County said at a news conference this week.

Along with her grief, Rebecca's mother, Tricia Norman, faces the frustration of wondering what else she could have done. She complained to school officials for several months about the bullying, and when little changed, she pulled Rebecca out of school. She closed down her daughter's Facebook page and took her cellphone away. She changed her number. Rebecca was so distraught in December that she began to cut herself, so her mother had her hospitalized and got her counseling. As best she could, Ms. Norman said, she kept tabs on Rebecca's social media footprint.

It all seemed to be working, she said. Rebecca appeared content at her new school as a seventh grader. She was gearing up to audition for chorus and was considering slipping into her cheerleading uniform once again. But unknown to her mother, Rebecca had recently signed on to new applications — ask.fm, and Kik and Voxer — which kick-started the messaging and bullying once again.

"I had never even heard of them; I did go through her phone but didn't even know," said Ms. Norman, 42, who works in customer service. "I had no reason to even think that anything was going on. She was laughing and joking."

Sheriff Judd said Rebecca had been using these messaging applications to send and receive texts and photographs. His office showed Ms. Norman the messages and photos, including one of Rebecca with razor blades on her arms and cuts on her body. The texts were full of hate, her mother said: "Why are you still alive?" "You're ugly."

One said, "Can u die please?" To which Rebecca responded, with a flash of resilience, "Nope but I can live." Her family said the bullying began with a dispute over a boy Rebecca dated for a while. But Rebecca had stopped seeing him, they said.

Rebecca was not nearly as resilient as she was letting on. Not long before her death, she had clicked on questions online that explored suicide. "How many Advil do you have to take to die?"

In hindsight, Ms. Norman wonders whether Rebecca kept her distress from her family because she feared her mother might take away her cellphone again.

“Maybe she thought she could handle it on her own,” Ms. Norman said.

It is impossible to be certain what role the online abuse may have played in her death. But cyberbullying experts said cellphone messaging applications are proliferating so quickly that it is increasingly difficult for parents to keep pace with their children’s complex digital lives.

“It’s a whole new culture, and the thing is that as adults, we don’t know anything about it because it’s changing every single day,” said Denise Marzullo, the chief executive of Mental Health America of Northeast Florida in Jacksonville, who works with the schools there on bullying issues.

No sooner has a parent deciphered Facebook or Twitter or Instagram than his or her children have migrated to the latest frontier. “It’s all of these small ones where all this is happening,” Ms. Marzullo said.

In Britain, a number of suicides by young people have been linked to ask.fm, and online petitions have been started there and here to make the site more responsive to bullying. The company ultimately responded this year by introducing an easy-to-see button to report bullying and saying it would hire more moderators.

“You hear about this all the time,” Ms. Norman said of cyberbullying. “I never, ever thought it would happen to me or my daughter.”

Questions have also been raised about whether Rebecca’s old school, Crystal Lake Middle School, did enough last year to help stop the bullying; some of it, including pushing and hitting, took place on school grounds. The same students also appear to be involved in sending out the hate-filled online messages away from school, something schools can also address.

Nancy Woolcock, the assistant superintendent in charge of antibullying programs for Polk County Schools, said the school received one bullying complaint from Rebecca and her mother in December about traditional bullying, not cyberbullying. After law enforcement investigated, Rebecca’s class schedule was changed. Ms. Woolcock said the school also has an extensive antibullying campaign and takes reports seriously.

But Ms. Norman said the school should have done more. Officials told her that Rebecca would receive an escort as she switched classes, but that did not happen, she said.

Rebecca never boarded her school bus on Monday morning. She made her way to the abandoned Cemex plant about 10 minutes away from her modest mobile home; the plant was a place she had used as a getaway a few times when she wanted to vanish. Somehow, she got past the high chain-link fence topped with barbed wire, which is now a memorial, with teddy bears, candles and balloons. She climbed a tower and then jumped.

"Don't ignore your kids," Ms. Norman said, "even if they seem fine."

LANCE SPEERE contributed reporting from Lakeland, Fla., and **ALAN BINDER** from Atlanta.

Meet Facebook's Mr. Nice

BY NICK BILTON | OCT. 22, 2014

OF FACEBOOK'S 7,185 EMPLOYEES, Arturo Bejar may have the most difficult job.

No, he is not responsible for increasing advertising revenue or keeping the website alive 24 hours a day. Mr. Bejar has a much more inscrutable task: teaching the site's 1.3 billion users, especially its tens of millions of teenagers, how to be nice and respectful to one another.

Respectful? Online? Ha! That's never going to happen. Everyone knows that social media is an unwinnable game of who can be meaner. If Mr. Bejar thinks he can make Facebook users nice, he is — to borrow a popular Facebook comment — just stupid!

But that kind of response is exactly what Mr. Bejar is counting on. As the director of engineering for the Facebook Protect and Care team, 80-strong, he believes that most users are not trying to be mean and that they will retract a comment (and even feel bad about it) if they realize it has caused someone harm.

"The way our brains work, we have evolved to understand each other by tone of voice or seeing facial expressions, but that gets lost through the devices we use to communicate," Mr. Bejar said last week in an interview at Facebook's New York offices.

In other words, Mr. Bejar is trying to create empathy among Facebook users, in what used to happen in real settings like the playground through social cues like crying and laughter.

This may seem like a piffling side project to some. But I believe the success of social media largely depends on solving this problem and teaching users to be kinder and more empathetic. Most people I know who have quit services like Twitter and Instagram have done so because commenters were spiteful, insensitive or just plain nasty.

According to a report released this week by Pew Research's Internet Project, 65 percent of young adults 18 to 29 in the United States said that they had been harassed online, and 92 percent had witnessed someone else being bullied.

But Facebook's efforts to curb this may be working. The company told me that each week eight million Facebook members use tools that allow users to report a harmful post or photo. (The tools can be used by clicking on the little upside-down arrow in the upper right corner of a post or the options button at the bottom of photos.)

Mr. Bejar's team designed these tools to let people know someone had hurt their feelings, and he said the system actually worked. (This is different from the newsfeed experiment in June, when Facebook received criticism for tinkering with people's emotions as part of a psychological study to examine how emotions can be spread on social media.)

Creating empathy on Facebook has not been easy. Researchers have learned that a few letters can have a profound impact. For example, in the first iteration of these tools, Facebook gave users a short list of vague emotions — like "embarrassing" — to communicate why they wanted a post removed. At the time, 50 percent of users seeking to delete a post would use the tool, but when Facebook added the word "it's" to create a complete sentence ("It's embarrassing"), the interaction shot up to 78 percent.

Teenagers are a particular focus, not just as victims of cyberbullying but because they sometimes lack the emotional maturity to handle negative posts.

Dr. Marc Brackett, director of the Yale Center for Emotional Intelligence, who is working with Facebook on this emotions project with the Protect and Care team, said their research found that teenagers need more pathways and options to voice their feelings.

On Facebook, teenagers are presented with more options than just "it's embarrassing" when they want to remove a post. They are asked what's happening in the post, how they feel about it and how sad they are. In addition, they are given a text box with a polite pre-written response that can be sent to the friend who hurt their feelings. (In early versions of this feature, only 20 percent of teenagers filled out the form. When Facebook added more descriptive language like "feelings" and "sadness," the figure grew to 80 percent.)

"We've played around with having pre-populated messages versus no message at all," Dr. Brackett said. "If kids are given a blank box, often times they are going to say things that are not going to be helpful," including cursing at their friends. When Facebook offered more developed responses like "This post is mean. It makes me feel sad and I don't want it on Facebook," 85 percent of teenagers who wanted a post removed sent a message.

"When kids let someone know they've hurt their feelings in a personal way, there's a strong likelihood that the other kid will take that down," Dr. Brackett said.

Interestingly, more often than not, the posts were not meant to hurt, but were jokes lost in digital translation. When Facebook asked people why they shared a post that hurt someone else, around 90 percent of respondents said they thought their friends would like the post or would think it was funny. Only 2 percent of users wanted to provoke or alarm someone else.

"Believe it or not, most of the time people do mean well," said Dacher Keltner, a director of the Greater Good Science Center at the University of California, Berkeley, who is also working with Facebook's empathy team.

Researchers are looking at other ways to help users be more empathetic on social networks. Last year, Facebook borrowed ideas from Charles Darwin's 1872 book, "The Expression of the Emotions in Man and Animals," to create stickers with facial expressions.

Next, Mr. Bejar said, his team is experimenting with sounds to help people convey how they feel. (Imagine sending someone the sound of a grunt, sigh or a giggle to communicate your feelings about a post.) But he acknowledged, "technology still has a lot of work to do to humanize each other."

Maybe this idea isn't that stupid after all.

CHAPTER 4

Parenting and Education

Parents and educators confront questions surrounding cyberbullying every day. How old is old enough to use social media? How can adults know when kids are encountering problems with online harassment, before it's too late? Is my child or student capable of writing the horrific kinds of comments I read online? Answers do not come easily, but discussing the questions is key.

Letting Your Kids Play in the Social Media Sandbox

BY NICK BILTON | FEB. 18, 2015

GIVEN MY LINE OF WORK, I am asked a lot of tech questions. What's the best cellphone to get for work? Should I upgrade my laptop? Can you come over to set up my router?

Then the other morning, a question stumped me. It was my 9-year-old nephew calling. "Erm, Uncle Nicky," Luca said slyly. "Can I have my own YouTube account?"

"What for?" I asked. Like many boys his age, he plays a lot of Minecraft, a virtual 3-D game, and he wanted to share videos of his gameplay with the real world. He asked his mom first, but she didn't know if it was appropriate. Hence, the call to me.

But I was just as befuddled. Sure, Luca would be able to post his videos to the world, but I also began to imagine Luca being attacked

JASON RAISH

and ridiculed in the comments section. Because, let's be honest, that's what the Internet mob does.

I told him I needed to think about it and call him back. "Awww," he said, clearly disappointed. "My friend Adam has one!" Unlike Barbies or Legos, there is no recommended age for letting your children play in the social media sandpit. There is no government-imposed age limit, like for consuming alcohol or driving. There is no parental guidebook (even if there was one, it would have to be updated weekly with each new social media upstart).

(Technically, most websites don't allow children under 13 to sign up for an account, as the Children's Online Privacy Protection Act, known as Coppa, prohibits companies from collecting information on children. But these rules are followed about as much as children adhering to PG-13 and R ratings for movies.)

After giving this some thought, both as an uncle and a tech columnist, here's where I draw the line today. When you break it down, there are essentially three social media doors that you can unlock for a child.

Behind Door No. 1 are public sites like Instagram, Twitter and YouTube, where by default everything anyone posts is visible to others. Some of these sites, along with Facebook, offer the ability to set content to "private," adding an extra level of protection. From a parent's perspective, this is good because you can still monitor every little thing your children share, and if they share too much, you can have a very uncomfortable talk about it.

Behind Door No. 2 are private apps like Snapchat and Telegram, where posts vanish after they are viewed. For parents, this means a child can share things without them ending up on search engines or being seen by unscrupulous people and advertisers. While this sounds safe, someone can easily take a screenshot of a picture or comment your child thought was private, then post it publicly. Then you can forget about college, marriage and grandchildren. (I kid, sort of.)

Then there is Door No. 3, with anonymous apps like Secret and YikYak that let people say anything they want, completely anonymously. For example, I could post "so-and-so is an idiot," and while so-and-so (and everyone else) could see it, there is no way to tie that comment back to me. Sounds fun, right? Not so much.

While these anonymous services can be helpful for children who want to express their feelings incognito, they also let cyberbullies thrive without repercussion. As a result, YikYak has become such a cesspool that it's been banned in a number of schools and there are online petitions to shut the app down. Going on Secret, another anonymous app, in its early days was like sticking your head in a sewage pipe.

Needless to say, I would caution parents from letting their children go behind the third door.

But what about the first two? I'll be the first to say that I'm not a parenting expert, but as someone who writes about the pros and cons of technology, I would be comfortable with letting children about 10 and older join public social media sites — with certain restrictions.

Children have much to gain from being on social media. They can learn how to communicate in today's connected world, and to find and share news and information. And sites like Instagram and YouTube allow them to be creative and share things they've made.

But parents should be vigilant in monitoring what their child posts. In the age of cyberbullying, it also offers a teachable moment. It is imperative that children learn that what they say online can hurt others. Teaching someone digital empathy is a dozen times more difficult than teaching them empathy in real life. And whether we like it or not, this is part of parenting today.

When your child is older, then they can graduate to the anonymous apps behind Door No. 2, where they can enjoy some privacy from snooping parents. But no matter how old they are, it's still important to talk to your children about being respectful on these services, and steering clear of those who are not. (I can think of a few adults who can benefit from that talk, too.)

A few other things: I'm a firm believer that parents should have the password to their children's account. Just like you can go into their room and check under the mattress, you should be able to go into their inbox, too. That doesn't mean you need to look, it just means you have the ability should something happen.

After giving it some thought, and seeking counsel from friends who work for social start-ups in Silicon Valley, I called Luca and told him that he could have a YouTube account, but with one big caveat. We would make his account settings private, so that no one could leave comments. He wasn't too happy about this, saying that no one, beyond his friends, would be able to tell him how wonderful his Oscar-worthy clips are.

"That's correct," I said. "And no one will be able to say anything mean to you, either."

You are probably thinking there is another option: Tell them to go outside and play. But then they would want to take photos and videos of that and post them to social media. Which would land us right back where we started.

When Your Child Is the Cyberbully

BY TARA PARKER-POPE | JUNE 29, 2010

THIS WEEK READERS submitted numerous questions about cyberbullying to our expert, Elizabeth K. Englander, a professor of psychology and the founder and director of the Massachusetts Aggression Reduction Center at Bridgewater State College, which provides anti-bullying and anti-violence training programs and resources to schools and families. This week, we'll begin posting her answers to selected questions.

Q: *We recently discovered several instances of one of my sons actually being the cyberbully. The transcripts were unbelievably obscene and I am devastated. I have had numerous talks with him about the severity of this issue, but I don't really understand what to do from there. We are turning off all free access to the computer for all the boys and are making them disable their social networking accounts. It is a shame for the others, but how could I know whether they are not doing the same kinds of things but are simply smarter about covering their tracks? Also, do we go to the parents of these girls he was harassing and let them know what happened? What is the right course? — Jim M.*

A: Dr. Englander responds:

First of all, I would like to take my hat off to you. How many countless times have we all seen parents who, faced with the evidence to the contrary, continue to insist that their own children are totally blameless? You are already more than halfway there, simply by virtue of your willingness to accept that your son made a mistake, and that you are the adult responsible for responding appropriately and ensuring that his mistake doesn't happen again.

Here are a few of my thoughts. First, I know the content of these types of communications are very upsetting. However, it's important to keep in mind that my own research in Massachusetts has found that children are significantly more willing to "go further" and to type very shocking things that they would never say in person. The fact that these communications occur in type, and online, greatly reduces their perceived impact. Kids believe that online statements simply "don't count" because they're not being said to someone's face. So please be partially reassured that this is likely the reason that the transcripts are as disturbing as they are.

Your reaction — to limit their social networking access — is probably the right one; but I would add one additional piece. Your son is going to have to learn how to use these communications appropriately, and to do that, he needs to practice. So I would emphasize to him that: (a) here are your expectations; and (b) if he wants to continue doing social networking in the future, he'll have to earn his way back to it by demonstrating consistently that he understands the rules, understands why they are important and can be relied upon to behave himself.

By adding these provisions, you're giving him some hope that he can regain his toys, but also underlining the importance of your rules. You can also let him know that regaining this privilege will occur only in stages; for example, the second stage might be letting him use a new Facebook account, but only with parental control software that (a) lets you see every single thing he types — no exceptions, and (b) limits the time he can spend on a site such as Facebook. As he progresses through the stages with no problems, you can ease up.

So what are your next steps?

First, you and he — together — need to work on his understanding of why cyberbullying is so wrong and hurtful. Have him read about, and discuss with him, the Phoebe Prince case and the Megan Meier case. Have him read newspaper stories and commentary online, and talk about the power of words. Don't be totally severe — it is fine to acknowledge that it can be tricky to know how your writing is taken, and that he may have meant to be funny or look "cool." Ask him to reflect upon why he did what he did, how he was feeling at the time, and what his motive was. Ask him to reflect upon what the impact was on his victim, and if this has ever happened to him.

Emphasize that his willingness to talk about this problem in a lengthy and meaningful way is part of how he is going to show you that he is reliable and can be trusted online. Give him a timeline, telling him, for example, "If you really take a lot of time to talk about this with me, and talk about it seriously, then in one month I'll reassess whether or not you can have limited access to Facebook." Note that this type of statement gives you a lot of "outs": the responsibility is really his to demonstrate his willingness to explore this issue. Don't worry if you sense that he's faking cooperation at first — it's not likely that after doing all this research, he'll be truly unaffected by all the damage and trauma surrounding this problem.

A final next step would be to consider reparations, which take into account the other family. As I've stated before, I'm not a lawyer, but I'll respond to this part of your question from a psychological point of view. Apologizing to the parents is a great idea, but don't expect them to be gracious about it, and let them know that you're not expecting that they'll just instantly forgive your son. Rather, let them know that you're calling to say that you're very sorry and that you are taking serious actions about the situation, and that you take it very seriously. Alternatively, you could just write them a letter, which might be easier for both you and them. I would hesitate, however, to advise you about having your son apologize to the target immediately. A victim of bullying can experience an apology as a veiled threat, even if it's not intended that way. That apology may be needed in future months, but for now, I would wait until you feel certain that your son has a handle on the situation.

It's hard for parents to acknowledge their own children's mistakes, but you are not the only parents dealing with this. In our research, 25 percent of kids told us they were cyberbullies. This is a problem many of us are going to have to learn to address. By owning up to the problem instead of denying it, you are well on your way.

As Bullies Go Digital, Parents Play Catch-Up

BY JAN HOFFMAN | DEC. 4, 2010

NINTH GRADE was supposed to be a fresh start for Marie's son: new school, new children. Yet by last October, he had become withdrawn. Marie prodded. And prodded again. Finally, he told her.

"The kids say I'm saying all these nasty things about them on Facebook," he said. "They don't believe me when I tell them I'm not on Facebook."

But apparently, he was.

Marie, a medical technologist and single mother who lives in Newburyport, Mass., searched Facebook. There she found what seemed to be her son's page: his name, a photo of him grinning while running — and, on his public wall, sneering comments about teenagers he scarcely knew.

Someone had forged his identity online and was bullying others in his name. Students began to shun him. Furious and frightened, Marie contacted school officials. After expressing their concern, they told her they could do nothing. It was an off-campus matter.

But Marie was determined to find out who was making her son miserable and to get them to stop. In choosing that course, she would become a target herself. When she and her son learned who was behind the scheme, they would both feel the sharp sting of betrayal. Undeterred, she would insist that the culprits be punished.

It is difficult enough to support one's child through a siege of schoolyard bullying. But the lawlessness of the Internet, its potential for casual, breathtaking cruelty, and its capacity to cloak a bully's identity all present slippery new challenges to this transitional generation of analog parents.

Desperate to protect their children, parents are floundering even as they scramble to catch up with the technological sophistication of the next generation.

Like Marie, many parents turn to schools, only to be rebuffed because officials think they do not have the authority to intercede. Others may call the police, who set high bars to investigate. Contacting Web site administrators or Internet service providers can be a daunting, protracted process.

When parents know the aggressor, some may contact that child's parent, stumbling through an evolving etiquette in the landscape of social awkwardness. Going forward, they struggle with when and how to supervise their adolescents' forays on the Internet.

Marie, who asked that her middle name and her own nickname for her son, D.C., be used to protect his identity, finally went to the police. The force's cybercrimes specialist, Inspector Brian Brunault, asked if she really wanted to pursue the matter.

"He said that once it was in the court system," Marie said, "they would have to prosecute. It could probably be someone we knew, like a friend of D.C.'s or a neighbor. Was I prepared for that?"

Marie's son urged her not to go ahead. But Marie was adamant. "I said yes."

PARENTAL FEARS

One afternoon last spring, Parry Aftab, a lawyer and expert on cyberbullying, addressed seventh graders at George Washington Middle School in Ridgewood, N.J.

"How many of you have ever been cyberbullied?" she asked.

The hands crept up, first a scattering, then a thicket. Of 150 students, 68 raised their hands. They came forward to offer rough tales from social networking sites, instant messaging and texting. Ms. Aftab stopped them at the 20th example.

Then she asked: How many of your parents know how to help you? A scant three or four hands went up.

Cyberbullying is often legally defined as repeated harassment online, although in popular use, it can describe even a sharp-elbowed, gratuitous swipe. Cyberbullies themselves resist easy categorization:

the anonymity of the Internet gives cover not only to schoolyard-bully types but to victims themselves, who feel they can retaliate without getting caught.

But online bullying can be more psychologically savage than schoolyard bullying. The Internet erases inhibitions, with adolescents often going further with slights online than in person.

"It's not the swear words," Inspector Brunault said. "They all swear. It's how they gang up on one individual at a time. 'Go cut yourself.' Or 'you are sooo ugly' — but with 10 u's, 10 g's, 10 l's, like they're all screaming it at someone."

The cavalier meanness can be chilling. On a California teenage boy's Facebook wall, someone writes that his 9-year-old sister is "a fat bitch." About the proud Facebook photos posted by a 13-year-old New York girl, another girl comments: "hideous" and "this pic makes me throwup a lil." If she had to choose between the life of an animal and that of the girl in the photos, she continues, she would choose the animal's, because "yeah, at least they're worth something."

This is a dark, vicious side of adolescence, enabled and magnified by technology. Yet because so many horrified parents are bewildered by the technology, they think they are helpless to address the problems it engenders.

"I'm not seeing signs that parents are getting more savvy with technology," said Russell A. Sabella, former president of the American School Counselor Association. "They're not taking the time and effort to educate themselves, and as a result, they've made it another responsibility for schools. But schools didn't give the kids their cellphones."

As bullying, or at least conflict, becomes more prevalent in the digital world, parents are beginning to turn out for community lectures, offered by psychologists, technology experts and the police. One weekday night this fall, Meghan Quigley, a mother from Duxbury, Mass., was among the 100 or so parents who attended a panel featuring Elizabeth Englander, a psychologist who consulted on the new Massachusetts bullying law.

"I absolutely have to be much more techno savvy than I want to be," said Mrs. Quigley, who does not know how to text, although two of her children use cellphones just to text their friends. "But it is overwhelming to me."

These lectures typically combine technology primers so elementary that elementary-school children might snicker, with advanced course work in 21st-century child-rearing.

Dr. Englander reminded parents that while children may be nimble with technology, they lack the maturity to understand its consequences.

Then she demonstrated how to adjust Facebook privacy settings. Many parents peered at her slides, taking notes.

Don't set too much stock in those settings, she said: " 'Privacy' is just a marketing term." A child's Facebook friend, she noted, could easily forward the "private" information.

In a study last year of 312 freshmen at Bridgewater State University, Dr. Englander found that 75 percent reported that during a typical high school day they had used their cellphones for voice communication 30 percent of the time or less, preferring to use them for texting, sending photos and videos, and surfing the Internet.

This is not a "phone," Dr. Englander told the parents who looked, collectively, shellshocked. What you've given your child "is a mobile computer."

If their children get caught in a crisis, she said, parents should preserve the evidence, by taking a screenshot of the offending material.

A mother timidly raised her hand. "How do I make a screenshot?"

THE BULLY NEXT DOOR

Throughout the fall, the Facebook profile set up in D.C.'s name taunted students: "At least I don't take pics of myself in the mirror like a homosexual midget," wrote "D.C." Also, "you smell weird." And "ur such a petaphile." At school, students would belligerently ask D.C. why he was picking fights on Facebook. He would eat lunch alone, and skipped some school, insisting that he was ill.

"I would always ask him, 'Are you having a good day?' " Marie said. "So he stopped talking to me about anything at school. He was afraid I would make more trouble for him. But the real victim was being ostracized more than the kids who were being bullied on his Facebook page."

She would call Inspector Brunault weekly. Last fall, the detective had to subpoena Facebook for the address of the computer linked to the forged profile. Then he had to subpoena Comcast, the Internet service provider, for the home address of the computer's owner.

Facebook has since made it simpler to report malicious activity. Although Facebook declined to make its head of security available for an interview, a spokesman replied by e-mail that if Facebook determines that a report of an impostor profile is legitimate, "We will provide a limited amount of data that helps the person take steps to repair his or her identity."

Finally, in January, Inspector Brunault told Marie he was getting close. He visited the home address supplied by Comcast. When he left, he had two more names and addresses.

A few weeks later, he called Marie.

Just before dinner, Marie broke the news to D.C. Two culprits were 14; one was 13. After learning the first two names, D.C. said: "Those guys have never liked me. I don't know why."

But the third boy had been a friend since preschool. His father was a sports coach of D.C.'s.

D.C. was silent. Then he teared up.

Finally, he said, "Do you mean to tell me, Mom, that they hate me so much that they would take the time to do this?"

Inspector Brunault asked the boys why they had done it. That summer, they replied, they had been reading Facebook profiles of people's dogs, which they found hilarious.

They decided to make up a profile. They picked D.C. "because he was a loner and a follower."

Although the police did not release the boys' names because they are juveniles, word seeped through town. In the middle of the night, Marie received anonymous calls. "They told me my son should just suck it up," she recalled. "They said he would be a mama's boy. They would rant and then they would hang up."

CONTACTING THE OTHER PARENT

After Marie learned the identities of her son's cyberbullies, she did not call their parents. She was so incensed that she communicated only through official go-betweens, like the police and prosecutors.

But some parents prefer to resolve the issue privately, by contacting the bully's family. Psychologists do not recommend that approach with schoolyard bullying, because it can devolve into conflicting narratives. With cyberbullying, a parent's proof of baldly searing digital exchanges can reframe that difficult conversation.

Parents who present the other parents with a printout of their child's most repugnant moments should be prepared for minimization, even denial.

Maj. Glenn Woodson's daughter, Sierra, has a shortened leg because of a congenital condition. One night, when she was in sixth grade, she received a text message showing a stick figure of her lying prostrate, eyes crossed out, another girl holding a bloody blade over the body. It had been sent by three girls in Sierra's grade.

Major Woodson, who lives on an Army base in Monterey, Calif., contacted the military police. They had a stern sit-down with the families of the three girls. Teachers held a workshop on cyberbullying. Two families apologized to the Woodsons.

Finally, the mother of the third girl, the instigator, called. " 'It isn't her fault,' she said to my wife," Major Woodson said. "The mom said: 'I think this is way overblown. My daughter is being punished and she's not the only one who did it.' "

The mother did not apologize.

What may be offensive in one household may be just a shoulder shrug in another.

In the San Francisco Bay Area, Christine, who, like many parents interviewed for this article asked that her last name not be used to protect her child's identity, selected a school for her daughter largely because it eschewed technology. But when her daughter was in sixth grade, a classmate e-mailed her links to pornography sites.

Christine called the boy's mother. "I asked her to get her son to stop," Christine said. "She apologized, and her son wrote us a letter of apology."

But the boy's father disagreed. "He refused to put limits on the kid," said Christine, who works in marketing. " 'Oh, no, he needs total freedom and he can use his best judgment.' "

When well-intentioned observers intervene, they can find themselves scorned.

Jill Brown, a Westfield, N.J., mother who lectures on cyberbullying through her company, Generation Text, saw something online that disturbed her: a Facebook group sniping at a young girl titled "I Stalk (name deleted) And Her Junior Boyfriend." The group had some 500 "friends."

The mother of a group founder was a friend of Ms. Brown's.

Ms. Brown suggested her friend look at the site. She asked her not to let her daughter know who blew the whistle. Her friend was polite but distant.

By the next day, "The girl had defriended me on Facebook," Ms. Brown said. "I texted her mother seven times. She ignored me."

Three weeks later, the friend stopped by Ms. Brown's house for a trunk show. When Ms. Brown asked what had happened to the Facebook group, the woman airily dismissed it as an adolescent joke.

Parent-to-parent confrontations can also backfire against the child.

In a small Western resort town, Gerrie's daughter, Michaela, 14, received an obscene, threatening text from a boy who was the star of her ski team. He accused Michaela of having told his girlfriend that he was secretly dating someone else and vowed to ruin Michaela's life.

Michaela stared at the cellphone, tears rolling down her face. She had not informed on him.

Gerrie's husband called the boy's mother. After seeing the corrosive text, the mother took away her son's cellphone for a week.

The boy made good on his threat. He spread a false rumor that his mother wouldn't allow him to race, and that Michaela's snitching was to blame. The news erupted on Facebook.

Ski team members ostracized Michaela. She rode the lifts by herself. Before team practices, she would quake and vomit.

"I did what I thought was right to help my daughter," said Gerrie, an art teacher, "and I only ended up making it worse. But when your kid gets a text like that, what are you supposed to do?"

Dr. Sabella, the former president of the American School Counselor Association, says that parents should meet in public places, like the library or a guidance counselor's office, rather than addressing the conflict by e-mail. And the reporting parents should be willing to acknowledge that their child may have played a role in the dispute. To ease tension, suggests Dr. Englander, an expert on aggression reduction, offer the cyberbully's parent a face-saving explanation.

Her model script?

"I need to show you what your son typed to my daughter online. He may have meant it as a joke. But my daughter was really devastated. A lot of kids type things online that they would never dream of saying in person. And it can all be easily misinterpreted."

When that conversation is handled deftly, parents can achieve a reasonable outcome. The 14-year-old daughter of Rolin, a Nashville musician, began a relationship with a boy in her church group. But soon his texts and Facebook comments turned sexually graphic and coercive. When she backed away, he tried to isolate her. At a church retreat, he surreptitiously sent texts from her phone to three of her friends, all boys, saying she didn't want to see them again.

She had no idea what he had done: he had deleted the text messages.

Those texts stunned her friends. Rolin pieced together what happened and blocked the boy's number on his daughter's phone. The boy simply borrowed his friends' phones. Rolin called the boy's parents, who agreed to sit down with both teenagers. "It would have been easier to send an e-mail," Rolin said. "And yes, it was sure awkward to be talking to this 14-year-old kid in front of his parents about what he wrote to my daughter. But we had the proof.

"My goal wasn't to polish my shotgun. It's not about a show of force but a show of presence. I said, 'If you want to be friends with her, you can't text her and you can't use another boy's phone.' "

The boy's father said Rolin had been easier on his son than the father would have been, had the roles been reversed.

Eventually, the relationship cooled on its own. "But I still have his number blocked on her phone," Rolin said.

WHEN THE BULLY IS YOUR CHILD

After the police arrested the boys who usurped D.C.'s identity, the parents wrote Marie awkward apology letters. Only one mother phoned, in tears.

No matter how parents see their children, learning of the cruelties they may perpetrate is jarring and can feel like an indictment of their child-rearing.

One afternoon two years ago, Judy, a recent widow in Palm Beach County, Fla., who had been finishing her college degree, helping a professor research cyberbullying, and working in an office, got a call from the middle school.

"Your daughter is involved in a cyberbullying incident," the assistant principal said. "Come down immediately."

Her daughter and two others had made a MySpace page about another middle-schooler, saying she was a "whore," with a finger pointing to her private parts. The young teenagers printed out copies and flung them at students.

Judy rushed to school. Her daughter, a sweet, straight-A student, was waiting in the guidance counselor's office, her arms crossed defiantly.

"I said to her, 'This is a human being,' " Judy recalled. " 'This girl will be destroyed for the rest of her life!' And my daughter just said: 'I don't care. It's all true.' And I bawled while she just sat there."

The school suspended Judy's daughter for three days.

"I did not call the target, I'm ashamed to say," Judy recalled. "I didn't know how to get hold of her. The school wouldn't give me her name, and my daughter wouldn't talk to me."

Once Judy got over her shock, she said, "I had to accept that my daughter had really done this and it was so ugly."

Judy took away her daughter's computer, television and cellphone for months. She tried talking with her. Nothing. There were weeks of screaming and slammed doors.

Meanwhile, the girl's grades dropped. She was caught with marijuana. Judy realized that her daughter had long been bottling up many family stressors: illness and death, financial worries, her mother's exhausting schedule. In reaction, the girl had been misbehaving, including doing the very thing her mother found so abhorrent: cyberbullying.

In time, as Judy took long walks with her daughter, the girl began to resemble the child Judy thought she had known.

When her daughter's grades improved, Judy bought her a puppy. "A lot of people will disagree with me," Judy said, "but I thought, this is a way for her to be responsible for something other than herself, something that would be dependent on her for all its needs."

The girl doted on the puppy. One day, Judy asked: " 'Would you want anyone to be mean to your dog? Throw rocks at Foxy?' "

Her daughter recoiled. Judy continued: " 'How do you think other parents feel when something mean happens to their children?' Then she broke down crying. That's when I think she finally understood what she had done."

SUPERVISOR OR SPY?

Should teenagers have the same expectation of privacy from parents in their online accounts that an earlier generation had with their little red diaries and keys?

Software programs that speak to parental fears are manifold. Parents can block Web sites, getting alerts when the child searches for them. They can also monitor cellphones: a program called Mobile Spy promises to let parents see all text messages, track G.P.S. locations and record phone activity without the child knowing.

Parents who never believed they would resort to such tactics find themselves doing so.

Christine, the Bay Area mother whose daughter was sent links to pornography, struggled with how to supervise her daughter online. The challenge was compounded because students in the girl's grade were playing sexualized Truth or Dare games. Her daughter had a leading role.

Christine cut off her daughter's Internet access for months, mandating that she write schoolwork by hand. Over time, the girl earned back computer privileges. Christine also moved her to a parochial school. Then her daughter went on Facebook.

"We didn't know much about Facebook," said Christine, "but we set up serious monitoring." One program limited computer time; another blocked certain sites. Christine even had her daughter's Facebook password, so she could read the girl's private messages.

That was how Christine discovered 82 exchanges between her daughter, a freshman, and a popular senior boy at the school. Her daughter offered him oral sex if he promised not to tell friends. The boy wrote back, "Would it be O.K. if I tell friends but not the ones at school?"

Christine's daughter now sees a therapist. Christine herself uses a keystroke logger, software that records everything her two daughters write and see on their home computer. "It's uncomfortable," Christine said. "But my older daughter has demonstrated less than zero common sense. The level of trust between us is much lower than I'd like it to be. But I also think she was relieved that we caught her.

"My younger daughter calls me a stalker. She says we mistrust her because of what her sister did. That's true. But my eyes are open, and I won't go back."

Studies show that children tend to side with Christine's younger daughter. Last April in an omnibus review of studies addressing youth, privacy and reputation, a report by the Berkman Center for Internet and Society at Harvard noted that parents who checked their children's online communications were seen as "controlling, invasive and 'clueless.' " Young people, one study noted, had a notion of an online public viewership "that excludes the family."

Conversely, studies show that more parents are heading in Christine's direction. A recent study of teenagers and phones by the Pew Research Center Internet and American Life Project said that parents regard their children's phones as a "parenting tool." About two-thirds said they checked the content of their children's phones (whether teenagers pre-emptively delete texts is a different matter). Two-thirds of the parents said they took away phones as punishment. Almost half said they used phones to check on their child's whereabouts.

Anne Collier, editor of NetFamilyNews.org, a parenting and technology news blog, noted that stealth monitoring may be warranted in rare cases, when a parent suspects a child is at serious risk, such as being contacted by an unknown adult.

But generally, she said, spying can have terrible repercussions:

"If you're monitoring your child secretly," Ms. Collier said, "what do you say to the kid when you find something untoward? Then the conversation turns into 'you invaded my privacy,' which is not what you intended to talk about."

Experts do not agree on guidelines about monitoring. But most concur on one principle:

"There is no one technology that will keep your kids safe," said Dr. Larry D. Rosen, a psychology professor at California State University, Dominguez Hills, who writes about raising a tech savvy generation. "The kids are smart enough to get around any technology you might use."

Dr. Englander installed keystroke logger software on her family computer. She uses it less as a monitoring device than as a means to teach her sons about digital safety. The Post-it on the family's computer reads: "Don't Forget That Mom Sees Everything You Do Online." She does not, in fact, check frequently. She just wants her boys to think before they hit the "send" button, so they understand that there is no privacy online, from her, or anyone.

Last spring, the Essex County, Mass., district attorney's office sent the three boys who forged D.C.'s Facebook identity to a juvenile diversion program for first-time nonviolent offenders.

If the boys adhere to conditions for a year, they will not be prosecuted. According to a spokesman, those conditions include: a five-page paper on cyberbullying; letters of apology to D.C. and everyone they insulted in his name on Facebook; attending two Internet safety presentations; community service; no access to the Internet except to complete schoolwork. Their computers must be in a public family space, not the bedroom.

Marie, who reports that D.C. has a new circle of friends and good grades, is reasonably satisfied with the sentencing conditions.

But compliance is another matter. She believes that at least one boy is already back on Facebook.

Overburdened school administrators and, increasingly, police officers who unravel juvenile cybercrimes, say it is almost impossible for them to monitor regulations imposed on teenagers.

As with the boys who impersonated D.C. online, a district attorney's spokeswoman said, "That monitoring is up to the parents."

A Curriculum to Strengthen Students Against Cyberbullying

BY VIJAI SINGH | JUNE 4, 2014

THE FACING HISTORY SCHOOL in New York City takes a unique approach to cyberbullying, based in part on its partnership with Facing History and Ourselves, a professional development organization that integrates the concepts of identity, community, responsibility, decision-making and participation into all aspects of its curriculum. By looking at case studies about social injustices, students try to understand the circumstances and decisions surrounding these events and then relate that back to their own experience and communities.

Last fall, I asked students at the school to describe their experiences with social media and bullying and how their thinking has evolved since freshman year — thanks in large part to their school.

"I would hang out with this group of girls and I guess there were other people that didn't like my friends so then it turned out that they didn't like me," said Dayanara Romero, 17, who experienced bullying during her sophomore year. Now a senior, Ms. Romero, said that at the time she was being called names in school and online. "It's horrible because they would list it on the Internet," she said, "so everybody thinks that's you when in reality they don't know who you are." Ms. Romero said she learned to trust the social workers in the school. "They would make meetings with me and those people and that would actually help," she said.

In the history class that I observed, students were discussing human trafficking. "We don't maybe see human trafficking here but there are behaviors associated with it," said Mark Otto, 33, assistant principal. "There's ideas of being a perpetrator, control, power, a victim, that we see," he said, "and so how do we make those connections for kids and help them understand that there are similar behaviors in different instances." The students apply the lessons of larger social issues to their own lives.

The curriculum also consists of an advisory period where each grade focuses on a different topic. Meeting four times a week over four years with the same group of students and the same adviser "is designed as a way of saying to students there's a space in the school for you to stop and think about these issues," said Daniel Braunfeld, 32, program associate for special projects at Facing History and Ourselves.

In the advisory period I observed, students were watching a video about a young girl who lived in the South during the 1960s and witnessed her parents attacking buses. "When we talk about standing up against injustice and all of our curriculum is surrounded by ways that individuals speak out against the wrongs that are happening, it kind of ingrains in the kids and they become these empathetic individuals," said Jeffrey Galaise, 32, special ed coordinator and a teacher of English and history.

The ultimate goal is to encourage students to be both good students as well as civic participants. "Cyberbullying is an amazing case study because it doesn't happen inside of the walls of the school," Mr. Braunfeld said. "So what we are hoping will happen is that the students are being given the tools and the perspective and the lens to look outside of their school community and say this is something that is happening to members of my community that is wrong and I have the tools to be able to address that."

Online Bullies Pull Schools Into the Fray

BY JAN HOFFMAN | JUNE 27, 2010

THE GIRL'S PARENTS, wild with outrage and fear, showed the principal the text messages: a dozen shocking, sexually explicit threats, sent to their daughter the previous Saturday night from the cellphone of a 12-year-old boy. Both children were sixth graders at Benjamin Franklin Middle School in Ridgewood, N.J.

Punish him, insisted the parents.

"I said, 'This occurred out of school, on a weekend,' " recalled the principal, Tony Orsini. "We can't discipline him."

Had they contacted the boy's family, he asked.

Too awkward, they replied. The fathers coach sports together. What about the police, Mr. Orsini asked.

A criminal investigation would be protracted, the parents had decided, its outcome uncertain. They wanted immediate action.

They pleaded: "Help us."

Schools these days are confronted with complex questions on whether and how to deal with cyberbullying, an imprecise label for online activities ranging from barrages of teasing texts to sexually harassing group sites. The extent of the phenomenon is hard to quantify. But one 2010 study by the Cyberbullying Research Center, an organization founded by two criminologists who defined bullying as "willful and repeated harm" inflicted through phones and computers, said one in five middle-school students had been affected.

Affronted by cyberspace's escalation of adolescent viciousness, many parents are looking to schools for justice, protection, even revenge. But many educators feel unprepared or unwilling to be prosecutors and judges.

Often, school district discipline codes say little about educators' authority over student cellphones, home computers and off-campus speech. Reluctant to assert an authority they are not sure they have, educators can appear indifferent to parents frantic with worry, alarmed by recent adolescent suicides linked to bullying.

Whether resolving such conflicts should be the responsibility of the family, the police or the schools remains an open question, evolving along with definitions of cyberbullying itself.

Nonetheless, administrators who decide they should help their cornered students often face daunting pragmatic and legal constraints.

"I have parents who thank me for getting involved," said Mike Rafferty, the middle school principal in Old Saybrook, Conn., "and parents who say, 'It didn't happen on school property, stay out of my life.' "

According to the Anti-Defamation League, although 44 states have bullying statutes, fewer than half offer guidance about whether schools may intervene in bullying involving "electronic communication," which almost always occurs outside of school and most severely on weekends, when children have more free time to socialize online.

A few states say that school conduct codes must explicitly prohibit off-campus cyberbullying; others imply it; still others explicitly exclude it. Some states say that local districts should develop cyberbullying prevention programs but the states did not address the question of discipline.

Judges are flummoxed, too, as they wrestle with new questions about protections on student speech and school searches. Can a student be suspended for posting a video on YouTube that cruelly demeans another student? Can a principal search a cellphone, much like a locker or a backpack?

It's unclear. These issues have begun their slow climb through state and federal courts, but so far, rulings have been contradictory, and much is still to be determined.

Benjamin Franklin Middle School conveys an earnest sweetness associated with an earlier era. Its 700 students attend classes in a low-slung building from the mid-'50s, complete with a bomb shelter and generous, shaded playing fields.

During cafeteria lunch duty, a guidance counselor runs a foosball tournament, attracting a throng of laughing, shouting boys. This year's school musical: "Guys and Dolls."

For all its charms, Benjamin Franklin, a sixth-through-eighth-grade school in a wealthy New Jersey suburb, also lives bluntly in the present. A sixth-grade girl dashes to class, wearing a turquoise T-shirt with bold sequined letters: "Texting Is My Favorite Subject." The seventh-grade guidance counselor says she can spend up to three-fourths of her time mediating conflicts that began online or through text messages.

In April, the burden of resolving these disputes had become so onerous that the principal, Mr. Orsini, sent an exasperated e-mail message to parents that made national news:

"There is absolutely NO reason for any middle school student to be part of a social networking site," he wrote. If children were attacked through sites or texting, he added, "IMMEDIATELY GO TO THE POLICE!" That was not the response that the parents of the girl who had received the foul messages had wanted to hear.

Mr. Orsini sighed, relenting. After all, the texts were angry and obscene, the parents horrified, the girl badly rattled.

"We can certainly talk to the boy," the principal said.

Investigating a complaint can be like stumbling into a sinkhole. Over the next few days, an assistant principal, Greg Wu; Mr. Orsini; a guidance counselor; a social worker and an elementary school principal were pulled into this one:

The sixth graders had "dated" for a week, before the girl broke it off. The texts she received that Saturday night were successively more sneering, graphic and intimidating.

But the exchanges shown to Mr. Orsini were incomplete. Before handing her phone to her parents, the girl erased her replies.

The boy claimed he was innocent, telling Mr. Wu he had lost his cellphone that Saturday. "Yeah, right," said Mr. Wu.

The boy insisted he had dropped it while riding his bicycle that April afternoon with his brother and his brother's friend, both fifth graders.

By Wednesday, the girl's father called Mr. Orsini. "How is this boy still in school, near my daughter? Why can't you suspend him?"

The boy was a poor student in language arts classes, yet the text messages were reasonably grammatical. Mr. Wu dictated a basic sentence for the boy to write down. It was riddled with errors.

Next, an elementary school principal interviewed the fifth-grade boys separately.

By Thursday, Mr. Orsini telephoned the girl's parents with his unsettling conclusion:

The boy had never sent the texts. The lost phone had been found by someone else and used to send the messages. Who wrote them? A reference or two might suggest another sixth grader.

The identity would remain unknown.

Mr. Orsini told the girl's shaken parents that, aside from offering her counseling, the school, which had already devoted 10 hours to the episode, could do no more. "They were still in so much pain," Mr. Orsini said. "They wanted us to keep investigating."

MIDDLE SCHOOL MISERY

Meredith Wearley, Benjamin Franklin's seventh-grade guidance counselor, was overwhelmed this spring by dramas created on the Web: The text spats that zapped new best friendships; secrets told in confidence, then broadcast on Facebook; bullied girls and boys, retaliating online.

"In seventh grade, the girls are trying to figure out where they fit in," Mrs. Wearley said. "They have found friends but they keep regrouping. And the technology makes it harder for them to understand what's a real friendship."

Because students prefer to use their phones for texting rather than talking, Mrs. Wearley added, they often miss cues about tone of voice. Misunderstandings proliferate: a crass joke can read as a withering attack; did that text have a buried subtext?

The girls come into her office, depressed, weeping, astonished, betrayed.

"A girl will get mad because her friend was friends with another girl," Mrs. Wearley said.

They show Mrs. Wearley reams of texts, the nastiness accelerating precipitously.

"I've had to bring down five girls to my office to sort things out," she said. "It's middle school."

Recently, between classes, several eighth-grade girls from Benjamin Franklin reflected about their cyberdramas:

"We had so many fights in seventh grade," one girl said. "None of them were face-to-face. We were too afraid. Besides, it's easier to say 'sorry' over a text."

Another concurred. "It's easier to fight online, because you feel more brave and in control," she said. "On Facebook, you can be as mean as you want."

Studies show that online harassment can begin in fourth grade. By high school, students inclined to be cruel in cyberspace are more technologically sophisticated, more capable of hiding their prints. But that is also when older students may be more resilient:

"By high school, youths are developing more self-confidence, engaged in extracurricular activities and focusing on the future," said Sameer Hinduja, a professor at Florida Atlantic University and an author of "Bullying Beyond the Schoolyard."

"Their identity and self-worth come from external things that don't revolve around social relationships."

But during middle school, he said, "Peer perception largely dictates their self-worth." With their erupting skin and morphing bodies, many seventh-grade students have a hard enough time just walking through the school doors. When dozens of kids vote online, which is not uncommon, about whether a student is fat or stupid or gay, the impact can be devastating.

While research shows that traditional at-school bullying is far more pervasive than cyberbullying, each type of hostility can now blur and bleed into the other. Jeff Taylor, principal of Frank Lloyd Wright Intermediate School in West Allis, Wis., wades into cyber-related conflicts at school several times each week.

Recently, a seventh-grade girl held a weekend birthday party and her jealous former friend showed up. By Tuesday night, the uninvited guest had insulted the birthday girl's dress on Facebook, calling it and the girl's mother cheap. The remarks were particularly wounding, because the birthday girl's family is not well-off.

By Wednesday, Mr. Taylor said, "There were rumblings about it in the cafeteria. When kids start posturing and switching lunch tables, you can tell." He and an assistant tried to calm them.

But the posturing continued online. A confrontation at school was planned, and the details were texted. On Friday, during the four minutes between seventh-grade lunch and the next period, 20 girls showed up in a hallway and began shrieking.

At least four adults pulled the girls apart and talked them down.

"We must have spent five or six hours on this, throughout the week," Mr. Taylor said. "We got to the bottom of that pain and rejection. I don't consider it a waste of time. But at 3:03 those buses were pulling out and you know that as soon as the girls got home, they'd be blasting away about it on Facebook."

Though resolving cyberwars can be slippery and time-consuming, some schools would like students to report them at the outset, before they intensify. But experts on adolescence note that teenagers are loath to tell adults much of anything.

Some students think they can handle the ridicule themselves. Or are just too embarrassed to speak up. Others fear that parents will overreact.

If the child is texting at school or has a Facebook page without permission, "and now they're being bullied on it," said Parry Aftab, executive director of WiredSafety.org, "they can't admit it to parents. The parents will take away the technology and the kids are afraid of that.

Or the parents will underreact. They'll say: 'Why read it? Just turn it off!' " The most threatening impediment to coming forward can be the cyberbully's revenge. Graffiti on a cyberwall can't be blacked out with a Sharpie.

Mindful of risks to students who report bullies, some school districts have created anonymous tip sites. At Benjamin Franklin, the staff has many ways to give students cover.

"When girls ask their friends, 'What were you doing in the guidance counselor's office?' " Mrs. Wearley said, "I tell them, just say 'Mrs. Wearley was fixing my schedule.' "

THE LEGAL BATTLES

Tony Orsini, the Ridgewood principal, learned about a devastating Facebook group last November, two months after it started.

"I had a 45-year-old father crying in my office," Mr. Orsini said. "He kept asking, 'Why would someone do this to my son?' "

A Facebook page had sprung up about the man's son, who was new in town. The comments included ethnic slurs, snickers about his sexuality and an excruciating nickname. In short order, nearly 50 children piled on, many of them readily identifiable. "Kids deal with meanness all the time and many can handle it," said Mr. Orsini, 38, a father of two children. "But it never lasts as long as it does now, online."

The boy could not escape the nickname. At soccer and basketball games around town, opposing players he'd never met would hoot: "Oh, you're that kid."

The boy began missing school. He became ill. After weeks, he reluctantly told his parents.

"We don't always get to address these problems until the damage is done," Mr. Orsini said.

Because the comments had been made online and off-campus, Mr. Orsini believed that his ability to intervene was limited.

Rulings in a handful of related cases around the country give mixed signals.

A few families have successfully sued schools for failing to protect their children from bullies. But when the Beverly Vista School in Beverly Hills, Calif., disciplined Evan S. Cohen's eighth-grade daughter for cyberbullying, he took on the school district.

After school one day in May 2008, Mr. Cohen's daughter, known in court papers as J. C., videotaped friends at a cafe, egging them on as they laughed and made mean-spirited, sexual comments about another eighth-grade girl, C. C., calling her "ugly," "spoiled," a "brat" and a "slut."

J. C. posted the video on YouTube. The next day, the school suspended her for two days.

"What incensed me," said Mr. Cohen, a music industry lawyer in Los Angeles, "was that these people were going to suspend my daughter for something that happened outside of school." On behalf of his daughter, he sued.

Last November, Judge Stephen V. Wilson of Federal District Court found that the off-campus video could be linked to the school: J. C. told perhaps 10 students about it; the humiliated C. C. and her mother showed it to school officials; educators watched it and investigated.

But the legal test, he wrote in his 57-page decision, was whether J. C.'s video had caused the school "substantial" disruption. Judge Wilson ruled in favor of the young videographer, because the disruption was only minimal: administrators dealt with the matter quietly and before lunch recess.

This legal test comes from a 1969 Supreme Court case, Tinker v. Des Moines Independent Community School District, in which a school suspended students for wearing black armbands to protest the Vietnam War.

The court overturned the suspension, but crafted a balance between a school's authority and a student's freedom of expression. When a student's speech interferes substantially with the school's educational mission, a school can impose discipline.

The district had to pay J. C.'s costs and lawyers' fees: $107,150.80.

Judge Wilson also threw in an aside that summarizes the conundrum that is adolescent development, acceptable civility and school authority.

The good intentions of the school notwithstanding, he wrote, it cannot discipline a student for speech, "simply because young persons are unpredictable or immature, or because, in general, teenagers are emotionally fragile and may often fight over hurtful comments."

The lesson Mr. Cohen hopes his daughter learns from the case is about the limits on governmental intrusion. "A girl came to school who was upset by something she saw on the Internet," Mr. Cohen said in a telephone interview, "and these people had in their mind that they were going to do something about it. The school doesn't have that kind of power. It's up to the parents to discipline their child."

He did chastise his daughter, saying, "That wasn't a nice thing to do."

He describes her video as "relentlessly juvenile," but not an example of cyberbullying, which he said he did not condone. His daughter offered to remove it from YouTube. But Mr. Cohen keeps it posted, he said, "as a public service" so viewers can see "what kids get suspended for in Beverly Hills."

The J. C. decision has ignited debate. Nancy Willard, an Oregon lawyer who consults with schools, said that the judge could have applied another, rarely cited prong of the Tinker standard: whether the student's hurtful speech collided with "the rights of other students to be secure."

The Supreme Court has not yet addressed online student speech. Lower-court judges in some districts have sided with schools that have disciplined students for posting threatening videos about educators from their home computers.

In two recent cases, students were suspended for posting parodies of their principals. Each case reached the Court of Appeals for the Third Circuit. But one three-judge panel sided with a school for disciplining a student whose site suggested the principal was a pedophile; another panel sided with its case's student, whose site suggested the principal used steroids and smoked marijuana. To resolve the contradictory rulings, both cases were re-argued earlier this month before 14 judges on the Third Circuit, whose jurisdiction includes New Jersey, Delaware, Pennsylvania and the United States Virgin Islands.

Nationwide, principals have responded to students who demean others online in dramatically different ways.

In January, 28 Seattle middle school students who wrote noxious comments on Facebook about one student received suspensions. The school also held assemblies about digital citizenship.

But when the mother of a seventh-grade boy in Fairfax County, Va., who requested anonymity to protect her son's identity, sent his principal the savage e-mail messages and Facebook jeers that six boys posted about her son, the principal wrote back that although the material was unacceptable, "From a school perspective this is outside the scope of our authority and not something we can monitor or issue consequences for."

Many principals hesitate to act because school discipline codes or state laws do not define cyberbullying. But Bernard James, an education law scholar at Pepperdine University, said that administrators interpreted statutes too narrowly:

"Educators are empowered to maintain safe schools," Professor James said. "The timidity of educators in this context of emerging technology is working to the advantage of bullies."

Whether suspension is appropriate is also under discussion. Elizabeth Englander, a psychology professor at Bridgewater State College in Massachusetts and founder of the Massachusetts Aggression Reduction Center, believes that automatic discipline for cyberbullies is wrong-headed.

"We tend to think that if there's no discipline, there's no reaction," she said. "But discipline should never be the only thing we consider in these cases. There are many things we can do with children first to guide and teach them about behavior and expectations."

Tony Orsini wanted to help his middle school student who was being teased mercilessly on Facebook. But he believed he had to catch the bullies at school.

He alerted teachers. At lunch, they spotted the three ringleaders as they forced the boy from their table.

"I called them into my office," Mr. Orsini said, "and talked to them strongly about the lunchroom incident. Then I lied. I said I heard that the cops were looking at a Facebook group they had posted.

"It came down the next day."

He rubbed his face in his hands. "All we are doing is reacting," he said. "We can't seem to get ahead of the curve."

GATHERING EVIDENCE

Administrators who investigate students tangled in online disputes often resort to a deft juggle of artfulness, technology and law.

First challenge: getting students to come clean.

Mr. Wu, the assistant principal at Benjamin Franklin, is a former household handyman and English teacher with a fondness for scraps, gadgets and imagination. Hence his lie detector:

It's really an ancient tuner, connected to a helmet labeled "The Anti-Prevaricator" — the inner webbing from a football helmet refurbished by Mr. Wu, who glued on bells and a keypad from an old telephone.

When students balk or obfuscate, Mr. Wu may suggest they don the Anti-Prevaricator. They answer questions; sparks flash from the tuner.

When sixth graders realize the joke, Mr. Wu said, "they start laughing with relief and we talk about the importance of telling the truth."

He continues his cyberinvestigations the old-fashioned way, with conversations, confrontations, cajoling and copious handwritten notes.

But the second challenge is gathering the evidence itself: looking at material typed on personal cellphones or online accounts.

School officials have both greater and lesser investigative authority than the police have over students. Certainly they cannot use lie detectors. But though police officers need probable cause and a warrant to search a student's locker or backpack, school administrators need only "reasonable suspicion" that a school rule has been violated.

The police also need probable cause and a warrant to search social networking sites and cellphones. School officials are uncertain what they need.

"I can't look into Facebook accounts," said Jeff Taylor, the middle school principal from West Allis, Wis. If students or parents want him to see something online, "they have to show it to me or bring me a printout."

But Deb Socia, the principal at Lilla G. Frederick Pilot Middle School in Dorchester, Mass., takes a no-nonsense approach. The school gives each student a laptop to work on. But the students' expectation of privacy is greatly diminished.

"I regularly scan every computer in the building," Ms. Socia said. "They know I'm watching. They're using the cameras on their laptops to check their hair and I send them a message and say: 'You look great! Now go back to work.' It's a powerful way to teach kids: 'I'm paying attention, you need to do what's right.' "

Administrators are skittish about searching cellphones because of the increase in sexting, in which students have sent compromising photos of themselves. Principals fear being caught up in child pornography investigations. In these situations, they generally turn over cellphones to the police.

"The question of searching a cellphone is a gray area," said Mary Ann McAdam, an assistant principal at Governor Livingston High School in Berkeley Heights, N.J. "We only do it when a student says, 'so-and-so sent threatening messages.' Even then, they look through their phones and find it for us. If I felt there might be something on a cellphone, I'd invite parents to go through it with me."

Legal experts disagree on this issue. Professor James argues that cellphones are like backpacks: if the search's purpose is reasonably related to a school infraction, like cheating, the principal's search is legal. Others believe that cellphones belong in another category, protected by electronic communication privacy laws.

While a cellphone search may yield an incriminating text, it may not point to the author.

Last year, an eighth-grade girl at Benjamin Franklin vowed on Facebook that her boyfriend would beat up another eighth grader, a girl she had been bullying throughout middle school. Mr. Orsini called the police.

Mr. Orsini ordered the girls to have no contact at school. Nonetheless, the bullied girl received veiled texted threats at school, sent from a phone owned by a friend of the bully. "Everyone knows who did it," said Mr. Orsini, looking miserable. "But I couldn't prove who really sent them. So I had to punish the girl whose phone was used. The bully was a masterful manipulator. Her friend took the hit for her."

By now, the targeted girl had become more self-confident. She was furious that the bully escaped punishment. When the bully began picking on a second, weaker girl, she grew further incensed.

One bristling morning, the two girls came to blows, which the bully sorely came to regret. Although teachers quickly broke up the fight, word of the outcome spread more swiftly:

"All the kids chanted the victim's name," Mr. Orsini said, "in triumph in the lunchroom."

THE CYBERSAGES

What a difference a few years can make in the life of a tween.

Earlier this month, a proud posse of Benjamin Franklin eighth-grade girls strode into homerooms of sixth graders: inches taller than the 12-year-olds, skin calmer, they radiated a commanding exuberance as they tossed their long, glossy manes. They wanted to offer advice about social networking sites and cyberbullying.

"How many of you have discussed Mr. Orsini's letter with your parents?" asked Annie Thurston, one of the eighth graders, referring to his admonitions about online activity.

Slumped in their desks, at least a dozen students in one class glumly hoisted their hands.

In April, a parent alerted Mr. Orsini about Formspring, a site on which comments can be sent anonymously to mailboxes, and posted at the mailbox owner's discretion. Many adults seem confounded at why girls, in particular, would choose to post the leering, scabrous queries; some teenagers say they do so in order to toss back hard-shelled, tough-girl retorts.

The principal found the names of some Benjamin Franklin students on Formspring. As Mr. Orsini later recounted the experience, he couldn't bring himself to utter even a sanitized version of the obscene posts he had read. His face reddened, tears filling his eyes.

"How does a 13-year-old girl recover her sexual self-esteem after reading that garbage?" he whispered.

It prompted his e-mail message to parents, in which he wrote that no middle school student needed to be on social networking sites. Many parents agreed. But others said that schools and families should work harder to teach students digital responsibility.

These eighth-grade girls thought Mr. Orsini was right: younger students shouldn't be on Facebook.

They grilled the sixth graders, almost all of whom said they had cellphones. Do your parents read your texts, they asked.

Only a smattering of palms.

"My mom keeps threatening to get software so she can monitor them," one boy said, shrugging his shoulders. "But she never gets around to it."

What impact did Mr. Orsini's letter have?

"I lied to my parents," another boy said. "I told them I deactivated my Facebook page. But in two days, I started it again."

The girls looked solemn.

"If you're under 13, you shouldn't even be on Facebook," said Maeve Cannon, 14. "We think you guys can handle it but you're still really young. It's not that necessary, you know. We just want you to be safe."

The sixth graders were rapt.

"The Internet is a scary place," said Sabrina Spatz, an eighth grader. "It can really hurt you. Our parents didn't grow up with it so they don't really understand it that well."

So if any of the sixth graders were cyberbullied, the older girls said, "Just come talk to us."

Then they hesitated. They were, after all, about to graduate.

"You can tell Mr. Wu, he's awesome!" said Maeve, bubbling over. "Tell your guidance counselor or a teacher." The other girls nodded eagerly.

"Yeah, go to the school," Emily Cerrina chimed in.

"The school will make it stop," she said, "immediately!"

Warily, Schools Watch Students on the Internet

BY SOMINI SENGUPTA | OCT. 28, 2013

SAN FRANCISCO — For years, a school principal's job was to make sure students were not creating a ruckus in the hallways or smoking in the bathroom. Vigilance ended at the schoolhouse gates.

Now, as students complain, taunt and sometimes cry out for help on social media, educators have more opportunities to monitor students around the clock. And some schools are turning to technology to help them. Several companies offer services to filter and glean what students do on school networks; a few now offer automated tools to comb through off-campus postings for signs of danger. For school officials, this raises new questions about whether they should — or legally can — discipline children for their online outbursts.

The problem has taken on new urgency with the case of a 12-year-old Florida girl who committed suicide after classmates relentlessly bullied her online and offline.

Two girls — ages 12 and 14 — who the authorities contend were her chief tormentors were arrested this month after one posted a Facebook comment about her death.

Educators find themselves needing to balance students' free speech rights against the dangers children can get into at school and sometimes with the law because of what they say in posts on Facebook, Twitter and Tumblr. Courts have started to weigh in.

In September, a federal appeals court in Nevada, for instance, sided with school officials who suspended a high school sophomore for threatening, through messages on Myspace, to shoot classmates. In 2011, an Indiana court ruled that school officials had violated the Constitution when they disciplined students for posting pictures on Facebook of themselves at a slumber party, posing with rainbow-colored lollipops shaped like phalluses.

"It is a concern and in some cases, a major problem for school districts," said Daniel A. Domenech, executive director of the American Association of School Administrators, which represents public school superintendents.

Surveillance of students' online speech, he said, can be cumbersome and confusing. "Is this something that a student has the right to do, or is this something that flies against the rules and regulations of a district?"

Interviews with educators suggest that surveillance of students off campus is still mostly done the old-fashioned way, by relying on students to report trouble or following students on social networks. Tracking students on social media comes with its own risks: One principal in Missouri resigned last year after accusations that she had snooped on students using a fake Facebook account. "It was our children she was monitoring," said one Twitter user who identified herself as Judy Rayford, after the news broke last year, without, she added, "authorization" from children or parents.

But technology is catching on.

In August, officials in Glendale, a suburb in Southern California, paid Geo Listening, a technology company, to comb through the social network posts of children in the district. The company said its service was not to pry, but to help the district, Glendale Unified, protect its students after suicides by teenagers in the area.

Students mocked the effort on Twitter, saying officials at G.U.S.D., the Glendale Unified School District, would not "even understand what I tweet most of the time, they should hire a high school slang analyst #shoutout2GUSD."

"We should be monitoring gusd instead," one Twitter user wrote after an instructor was arrested on charges of sexual abuse; the instructor pleaded not guilty.

Chris Frydrych, the chief executive of Geo Listening, based in Hermosa Beach, also in Southern California, declined to explain how his company's technology worked, except to say that it was "a sprinkling of technology and a whole lot of human capital." He said Geo Listening looked for keywords and sentiments on posts that could be viewed publicly. It cannot, for instance, read anyone's Facebook posts that are designated for "friends" or "friends of friends."

But with Facebook's announcement this month that teenagers will be permitted to post public status updates and images, Geo Listening and similar services will potentially have access to more information on that social network.

Glendale has paid Geo Listening $40,500 to monitor the social media posts. Mr. Frydrych declined to say which other schools his company works with, except to predict that by the end of the year, his company would have signed up 3,000 schools.

David Jones of CompuGuardian, based in Salt Lake City, said his product let school officials monitor whether students were researching topics like how to build bombs or discussing anorexia. His customers include five schools, but he, too, is optimistic about market growth.

"It helps you boil down to what students are having what problems," he said. "And then you can drill down."

But when does protecting children from each other or from themselves turn into chilling free speech?

John G. Palfrey Jr., head of Phillips Academy in Massachusetts, said he favored a middle ground. He follows his students on Twitter if they follow him, for instance, but he is wary of automated tools that try to conduct what he called National Security Agency-style surveillance.

He briefly contended with this question last year when students created a blog where they could anonymously share "secrets." Many posts were on the fringe, Mr. Palfrey recalled, and some teachers and students were concerned that children's identities could be determined from their writing patterns. The blog's student founders were persuaded to add a note of caution, warning participants that their identities could be discovered.

Mr. Palfrey offered an offline analogy. "We wouldn't want to record every conversation they are having in the hallway," he said. "The safety and well-being of our students is our top priority, but we also need for them to have the time and space to grow without feeling like we are watching their every move."

That fine line seems to be equally confounding the courts.

In the Nevada case, a 16-year-old boy bragged on Myspace about having guns at home, and threatened to kill fellow students on a particular date. He also cited the 2007 massacre at Virginia Tech, in which a troubled student killed 32 people.

The boy ended up spending 31 days in a local jail and was suspended from school for 90 days. He then sued the district, saying his free speech rights had been violated.

The Ninth Circuit Court of Appeals dismissed the claim. It called his threats "alarming" and so specific that they presented "a real risk of significant disruption" to the school. Administrators were justified, the court ruled, for penalizing what was ostensibly off-campus speech.

"It's going to be more and more of legal issues," said Gretchen Shipley, a lawyer who represents school districts. "The ability to monitor is growing so quickly."

The Indiana case offers a contrast. In the summer of 2009, two incoming 10th graders at Churubusco High School posted what the court called "raunchy" pictures of themselves. Once school officials found out, the girls were suspended from extracurricular activities for the school year. The girls sued, saying their free speech rights had been violated. The school contended that its student handbook bars conduct that could "discredit" or "dishonor" it.

The court found that prohibition too broad. The students' pictures, "juvenile" though they were, did not cause "substantial disruption" at school, the court ruled, and even though it was just "crude humor," it was protected speech. "No message of lofty social or political importance was conveyed, but none is required," the court said.

Questions for School on Bullying and a Suicide

BY ERIK ECKHOLM AND KATIE ZEZIMA | APRIL 1, 2010

SOUTH HADLEY, MASS. — On one point, everyone here agrees: the high school students who taunted and threatened Phoebe Prince for three months, until she hanged herself, deserve to be punished.

But acrimony over what school officials knew and how they dealt with the bullying of Ms. Prince, 15, has intensified since Monday, when the district attorney announced that six students who hounded her would face criminal charges.

School leaders said the district attorney had gotten it wrong when she said that teachers and officials had long known about the hazing of Ms. Prince, a newcomer from Ireland who was relentlessly taunted as an "Irish slut" by some students after she briefly dated a popular senior football star.

The district attorney, Elizabeth D. Scheibel, for her part, issued a terse statement on Thursday suggesting that the school superintendent did not know the facts. Lending support to the district attorney's account, some students said in interviews that they had seen teachers witness bullying incidents or had seen a teacher console Ms. Prince as she wept. On the day she committed suicide in mid-January, she was seen crying in the nurse's office, according to students.

As new details emerged about Ms. Prince's persecution, school district leaders, in a flurry of television appearances and interviews, insisted that neither they nor the principal had known the extent of the hazing. They said that teachers were instructed to report all incidents and that the principal of South Hadley High School learned only at the time about two examples of harassment of Ms. Prince, both about a week before her suicide, and had disciplined the two girls involved immediately.

Officials did not realize that several other girls continued to harass Ms. Prince in the days that followed, according to Gus Sayer, the superintendent, and Edward J. Boisselle, the chairman of the school committee, as the school board is known here. And only after her death, they said, did officials learn that she had been threatened and slurred since October.

The officials said they had no record of Ms. Prince's parents complaining to the school about the hazing, something that the district attorney and the parents say the mother did twice. They said they had taken districtwide measures to fight the problem of bullying well before Ms. Prince's torment came to light.

"We were proactive, but unfortunately, accidents and tragedies can still occur," Mr. Boisselle said in an interview.

Darby O'Brien, a friend of the Prince family, said Thursday that Ms. Prince's parents had told him that they had twice tried to alert the school and protect their daughter. Anne Prince, the mother, told him that in one case she had contacted a school official in November asking "whether this gang of girls was a threat to her daughter," and was told not to worry. The mother said she had contacted the school again in the first week of January as the taunting continued, Mr. O'Brien said.

The parents, who are discussing a possible civil suit, have refused to speak to reporters. Mr. O'Brien, a parent and head of an advertising agency here, called for the superintendent, board chairman and principal to resign. "I can't buy the story that they were unaware," he said. "They are running for cover."

Some parents defend the district. Jana Darrow-Rioux, who has been involved with the antibullying efforts started at the school last year, says she believes that the school is being unfairly blamed.

"I think it's convenient for people to want to punish the school because it's the only tangible organization in this mess," Ms. Darrow-Rioux said. She said that officials had not been able to share information during the investigations and that this had fueled unwarranted rumors.

In interviews, some students and parents described bullying incidents that they said were witnessed by teachers. A few times in

December and early January, for example, Ms. Prince arrived at a class late and crying; a teacher tried to console her in the hallway and then left her there, said a student who did not want to be identified, citing the criminal proceedings.

Susan Smith said that her son had watched as one of the accused bullies screamed insults in Ms. Prince's face in the cafeteria while the teenager tried to ignore it — and that two teachers saw the verbal assault but did not act.

Questions continued to swirl about the case.

On Thursday, the district attorney, Ms. Scheibel, said in a statement: "I do not intend to address Superintendent Sayer's assertions point by point. I will, however, say that Mr. Sayer does not have access to our investigative materials. Therefore he can't have a basis for some of his comments."

Some parents questioned the effectiveness of the school's internal investigation after Ms. Prince's death and what they described as a failure to discipline some of the offenders until the charges emerged this week.

"They had eyewitnesses to the bullying that they never interviewed," Ms. Smith said.

Some of the students who were accused were "removed from the school" this year, school officials said. Citing privacy rules, they would not say whether the students were suspended, expelled or sent to a different school.

But a few of them, school officials acknowledged, were removed only this week, after the announcement of charges against the six.

The various charges include statutory rape for the two boys, criminal harassment, violation of civil rights, stalking and other similar crimes.

The Princes lived in a small town in County Clare, Ireland, and Ms. Prince attended a boarding school in Limerick. The family had relatives in South Hadley, a region thick with Irish heritage, and decided to move here last year.

The mother, a schoolteacher, brought Ms. Prince and her 12-year-old sister to Massachusetts, renting the top floor of a house near the high school while their father stayed behind to sell their house.

By all accounts a lively girl, newly arrived at school last fall with an Irish brogue, Ms. Prince soon caught the eye of Sean Mulveyhill, a senior and a football star, and they briefly dated.

But Mr. Mulveyhill, 17, also dated Kayla Narey, 17, who like him was a longtime resident and part of a popular clique at the school, according to a friend of the students. He cut ties with Ms. Prince, and Ms. Narey and some of her friends started their campaign against her in October, students said. Mr. Mulveyhill and Ms. Narey have been charged.

Around the same time, other girls, including Flannery Mullins, 16, and Sharon Chanon Velasquez, 16, both of whom were charged, started harassing Ms. Prince, students said.

Some girls cursed Ms. Prince when they saw her in the hallways or cafeteria, shouting epithets and sometimes, in the library, whispering them as they went by.

"People were calling her a druggie or a slut, and she immediately got this horribly bad reputation," said Betty Czitcom, a sophomore.

They vilified her on Web sites and sent her text messages calling her a slut and a whore and telling her she deserved to die, according to Ms. Prince's friends.

On the afternoon of her death, on Jan. 14, other students said they saw Ms. Prince going into the nurse's office, crying. A school official confirmed that Ms. Prince had seen the nurse but said he could not comment on the reasons.

After 2 p.m., as Ms. Prince walked the three blocks to her home, girls from the younger group sped by and hit her with a can of Red Bull, according to friends of Ms. Prince.

Ms. Prince's younger sister found her at 4:30 p.m., hanging from the stairwell by the scarf her sister had given her for Christmas.

In the traumatic days that followed, Rebecca Brouillard, a student who spoke on a television interview about the hazing, was slammed against a wall and hit by one of the accused girls, said her father, Mitch Brouillard. He said that they were angry she had publicly discussed the bullying, and that some of the students who were accused had bullied his own daughter for years.

Dozens of parents attended a school committee meeting at the time and described a history of bullying at the school that many said had never been brought under control.

But school district officials noted that last fall, out of concern after the suicide of a boy in Springfield, Mass., they brought a leading consultant, Barbara Coloroso, to give a seminar about prevention and reporting of bullying.

Ms. Coloroso rushed back to South Hadley after Ms. Prince's death. She said in an interview this week that the high school had not fully carried out her recommendations to ensure reporting of any potential bullying and to involve parents early on.

"This was a horrible wake-up call," she said.

Melania Trump Wants to End Online Bullying. Her Husband Doesn't Help.

BY KATIE ROGERS | MARCH 20, 2018

WITH A PARTICULAR FOCUS on social media, Melania Trump, the first lady, has long said she wants to curb online bullying and harassment as part of a nascent effort to improve the lives of American children. There's one problem: Mrs. Trump's efforts often clash with the president's longtime habit of using social media to insult people.

Despite the criticism, she has continued to develop an agenda around cybersafety. On Tuesday, Mrs. Trump invited representatives from Facebook, Snap, Google, Amazon and Twitter to the White House for a round-table discussion on the topic. In a speech, she said that she had received letters from children who have been bullied or feel threatened on social media.

"I am well aware that people are skeptical of me discussing this topic," Mrs. Trump said on Tuesday. "I have been criticized for my commitment to tackling this issue, and I know that will continue. But it will not stop me from doing what I know is right. I am here with one goal: helping children and our next generation."

So far, Mrs. Trump is working on this initiative independently of her husband. On Tuesday, President Trump had already attacked Democrats. Here are other times his behavior on Twitter has clashed with her public remarks on the importance of curbing bullying.

FEB 26. 2018

Mrs. Trump

Days after visiting survivors of a mass school shooting in Parkland, Fla., Mrs. Trump addressed a group of governors' spouses at the White House. She offered support for students who were protesting against current gun laws, and brought up social media exposure as one of the "evils in our world today." Mrs. Trump said adults should take responsibility for monitoring children's behavior on social media.

"Before you leave to go back to your wonderful states and territories, I'm asking you all to join me today and commit to promoting values such as encouragement, kindness, compassion and respect in our children," Mrs. Trump said to the group. "With those values as a solid foundation, our kids will be better equipped to deal with many of the evils in our world today, such as drug abuse and addiction and negative social media interactions."

Mr. Trump

That week, Mr. Trump singled out Jeff Sessions, his attorney general, the investigation led by the special counsel and the state of California.

WITCH HUNT!

— Donald Trump (@realDonaldTrump) Feb. 28, 2018

Why is A.G. Jeff Sessions asking the Inspector General to investigate potentially massive FISA abuse. Will take forever, has no prosecutorial power and already late with reports on Comey etc. Isn't the I.G. an Obama guy? Why not use Justice Department lawyers? DISGRACEFUL!

— Donald Trump (@realDonaldTrump) Feb. 28, 2018

I have decided that sections of the Wall that California wants built NOW will not be built until the whole Wall is approved. Big victory yesterday with ruling from the courts that allows us to proceed. OUR COUNTRY MUST HAVE BORDER SECURITY!

— Donald Trump (@realDonaldTrump) Feb. 28, 2018

OCT. 23, 2017

Mrs. Trump

Mrs. Trump, in another public indication that she may refocus on efforts related to an early promise to combat cyberbullying, visited a middle school in a Detroit suburb. In between posing for selfies, she urged students to treat one another with respect and kindness.

"I encourage you to find a new friend and eat lunch with a new friend," Mrs. Trump told a group of seventh- and eighth-grade students who had gathered in the cafeteria with their lunchboxes, backpacks and smartphones. "I think it's very important to choose kindness and compassion."

Mr. Trump

That day, Mr. Trump attacked the National Football League in a continuing battle over players kneeling during the national anthem to protest police brutality, racism and the current state of the criminal justice system.

Two dozen NFL players continue to kneel during the National Anthem, showing total disrespect to our Flag & Country. No leadership in NFL!

— Donald Trump (@realDonaldTrump) Oct. 23, 2017

He also singled out the widow of a soldier killed in an ambush in Niger. Myeshia Johnson, whose husband, Sgt. La David T. Johnson, was killed, said the president had struggled to remember her husband's name during a phone call.

"The president said, 'He knew what he signed up for, but it hurts anyway,' " Ms. Johnson said during an interview with ABC News's George Stephanopoulos. "It made me cry because I was very angry at the tone in his voice and how he said it."

Mr. Trump used his preferred platform to hit back.

I had a very respectful conversation with the widow of Sgt. La David Johnson, and spoke his name from beginning, without hesitation!

— Donald Trump (@realDonaldTrump) Oct. 23, 2017

SEPT. 20, 2017

Mrs. Trump

In a speech at a United Nations luncheon, Mrs. Trump warned about the dangers to children posed by cyberbullying and drugs.

"We must turn our focus right now to the message and content they are exposed to on a daily basis through social media," Mrs. Trump said to a luncheon group. "The bullying, the experience online and in person and the growing global epidemic of drug addiction and drug overdose."

Mr. Trump

That week, Mr. Trump criticized several targets, including the leader of North Korea, the Emmys and Senator Rand Paul, Republican of Kentucky.

I was saddened to see how bad the ratings were on the Emmys last night - the worst ever. Smartest people of them all are the "DEPLORABLES."

— Donald Trump (@realDonaldTrump) Sep. 19, 2017

Rand Paul, or whoever votes against Hcare Bill, will forever (future political campaigns) be known as "the Republican who saved ObamaCare."

— Donald Trump (@realDonaldTrump) Sep. 22, 2017

Kim Jong Un of North Korea, who is obviously a madman who doesn't mind starving or killing his people, will be tested like never before!

— Donald Trump (@realDonaldTrump) Sep. 22, 2017

MAY 25, 2017

Mrs. Trump

During the president's first trip abroad, Mrs. Trump met with Queen Mathilde of Belgium and watched a presentation about a program that advocates for missing and exploited children. Mrs. Trump emphasized the need for digital safety after the meeting.

"It is so important that we talk to children about their online activities, to let them know that computers are useful tools but can be used by people who want to harm them," Mrs. Trump said in a statement released through the White House.

Mr. Trump

That week, the president was on his best Twitter behavior. He praised European leaders, called his meeting with Pope Francis "the honor of a lifetime" and discussed his poll numbers.

Honor of a lifetime to meet His Holiness Pope Francis. I leave the Vatican more determined than ever to pursue PEACE in our world.

— Donald Trump (@realDonaldTrump) May 24, 2017

Thank you for your support. Together, we will MAKE AMERICA SAFE AND GREAT AGAIN!#POTUSAbroad #USA

— Donald Trump (@realDonaldTrump) May 25, 2017

NOV. 3, 2016

Mrs. Trump

For the first time, Mrs. Trump said publicly that she wanted to help combat cyberbullying during a campaign stop in Pennsylvania.

"We have to find a better way to talk to each other, to disagree with each other, to respect each other. We must find better ways to honor and support the basic goodness of our children, especially in social media," Mrs. Trump said. "It will be one of the main focuses of my work if I'm privileged enough to become your first lady."

Mr. Trump

Needless to say, her critics pounced. For his part, Mr. Trump spent the week railing against his Democratic opponent, Hillary Clinton, and President Barack Obama.

ObamaCare is a total disaster. Hillary Clinton wants to save it by making it even more expensive. Doesn't work, I will REPEAL AND REPLACE!

— Donald Trump (@realDonaldTrump) Nov. 3, 2016

Looking at Air Force One @ MIA. Why is he campaigning instead of creating jobs & fixing Obamacare? Get back to work for the American people!

— Donald Trump (@realDonaldTrump) Nov. 3, 2016

On Tuesday, Carlos Monje, a representative from Twitter, the president's preferred digital soapbox, said the platform worked hard to "create a safe environment" for people 13 and older.

"Young people do come to Twitter to find community," he said. Adding, "We've seen some pretty inspirational things."

Over a year in the Trump presidency, the East Wing has not unveiled a formal policy initiative. On Tuesday, the East Wing did not give a timeline for a formal rollout. Stephanie Grisham, a spokeswoman for the first lady, said in an email that it was common for the East Wing to work independently of the West Wing on "some issues."

"It is, in fact, a huge part of life for children today and Mrs. Trump wants to use her platform to talk openly about how to use it in a positive way," Ms. Grisham said. "Of course she knows there is going to be criticism, but she is an independent woman who is doing what she feels is right for children. This should be celebrated, not criticized."

KITTY BENNETT contributed research.

Melania Trump Rolls Out 'Be Best,' a Children's Agenda With a Focus on Social Media

BY KATIE ROGERS | MAY 7, 2018

WASHINGTON — Hours after President Trump took to Twitter on Monday to denigrate the special counsel's investigation as a "Phony Witch Hunt" and the Iran deal as a "MESS," Melania Trump stepped into the Rose Garden and said she would focus her official effort as first lady on teaching children to put kindness first in their lives, particularly on social media.

In a speech delivered in front of her husband, Vice President Mike Pence, at least five cabinet secretaries and other senior officials, Mrs. Trump unveiled a program called "Be Best," which she said would tackle opioid abuse, social media pressures and mental health issues among young people.

"Children deserve every opportunity to enjoy their innocence," Mrs. Trump said.

Like the first lady herself, the full details of the plan were mysterious. Mrs. Trump's program will primarily repackage projects that already exist, including an initiative by the National Safety Council to encourage people to be proactive with talking to their doctors about opioid abuse, and guidelines distributed by the Federal Trade Commission on children's social media activity.

Mrs. Trump's staff plans to continue to solicit ideas from places the first lady has visited, including a West Virginia clinic that treats infants born with opioid addiction and a Michigan school where students participate in a program to stress the importance of emotional intelligence and kindness.

Kellyanne Conway, counselor to the president, has been a help briefing Mrs. Trump on the opioid crisis, a White House official said.

DOUG MILLS/THE NEW YORK TIMES

Melania Trump, the first lady, launched her "Be Best" initiative on Monday in the Rose Garden.

"We can and should teach children the importance of social and self-awareness, positive relationship skills and responsible decision making," Mrs. Trump said. "Let us teach our children the difference between right and wrong, and encourage them to be best in their individual paths in life."

Recent first ladies have poured their efforts into focused programs. Michelle Obama was an advocate for nutrition and fitness, Laura Bush championed literacy, Hillary Clinton pushed for health care, Barbara Bush promoted reading, Nancy Reagan started a "Just Say No" antidrug campaign and Rosalynn Carter sought to lift the stigma of mental illness. But Mrs. Trump has not narrowed her interests down to one issue and is instead broadly focused on helping children.

"There are too many critical issues facing children today for her to choose just one," her spokeswoman, Stephanie Grisham, said in an email about the first lady's plans. "She wants to use her platform as first lady to help as many children as she can."

In her speech, Mrs. Trump, who has remained media shy, delivered some of the longest public remarks she has as first lady. The event had a festive air: Under a sweltering afternoon sun in the Rose Garden, a military band played "I Wish" by Stevie Wonder before Mrs. Trump's remarks and "Change the World" by Eric Clapton afterward. Guests snacked on cookies emblazoned with "Be Best" in red and blue.

Mrs. Trump came up with the logo and program name herself, her aides said.

Observers on social media seized on the event, noting that the link the White House sent out for the "Be Best" website initially delivered an error message, and that Mrs. Obama, Mrs. Trump's immediate predecessor, had delivered a speech last year urging men to "be better." During the 2016 campaign, Mrs. Trump took flack for a speech that appeared to be sourced, in part, from remarks Mrs. Obama made in 2008.

Initially, Mrs. Trump had backed away from her original promise to combat cyberbullying after the criticism leveled at Mr. Trump for his online insults. Knowing she would get criticized if she pursued anything related to social media, Mr. Trump suggested she take an easier path. But Mrs. Trump ultimately decided to make good online behavior a part of something broader, an East Wing official said.

Mr. Trump appeared pleased. "That was truly a beautiful and heartfelt speech," he said in remarks in the Rose Garden after Mrs. Trump spoke. "It's the way she feels, very strongly. America is truly blessed to have a first lady who is so devoted to our country."

In her brief time at the White House — Mrs. Trump moved to Washington with her son, Barron, last June — she took her time establishing her own profile, with only a stilettoed misstep or two, literally: She piqued the public's interest by wearing high heels on a trip to Texas after it was hit by Hurricane Harvey. She also drew positive attention for speaking against the racial violence in Charlottesville, Va., that left one woman dead.

In January, after news broke that Stephanie Clifford, the pornographic film actress known as Stormy Daniels, was paid $130,000 before the 2016 election to keep quiet about a sexual encounter with Mr. Trump, Mrs. Trump cut back her public appearances. Her office dismissed her absence as a coincidence, while others close to the president said that Mrs. Trump had been angered by the news reports.

In recent months, Mrs. Trump has emerged more often without Mr. Trump by her side, although she has twice been seen avoiding or swatting the president's hand away during public appearances. She is rolling out her platform even as Mr. Trump and his legal team have added new, confusing contours to the story surrounding Ms. Clifford.

If Mrs. Trump remains something of an enigma to most Americans, there is at least some evidence that the public has warmed to the wife of a president whose popularity remains at historic lows. In a CNN poll conducted May 2 to May 5, 57 percent of respondents said they held a favorable view of Mrs. Trump — up 10 percentage points from January — while 27 percent had a negative view.

She is still less popular than her two predecessors during the second year of their husbands' terms: Mrs. Obama was viewed positively by 66 percent and negatively by 25 percent, according to a July 2010 Gallup poll, while Laura Bush was viewed positively by 67 percent and negatively by 8 percent, according to a May 2002 CNN/Time poll.

Yet the public has glimpsed less of Mrs. Trump than it had of the women who held the position before her. Brigitte Macron, the wife of President Emmanuel Macron of France, seemed to capture some of the challenges of her role when she commented that the American first lady was essentially trapped in the White House. "Melania can't do anything, she can't even open a window in the White House," Mrs. Macron told the French newspaper Le Monde. "She can't put her nose out."

One person close to Mrs. Trump said that, like other modern first ladies, she has chafed against some of the boundaries of living in the White House. But, that person said, she has begun to embrace the possibilities of her role, particularly because she has been touched by letters she has received from children who have been bullied. According to two others who know her, she has adjusted to the role primarily because her 12-year-old son is happy in Washington.

"She's a devoted mother," Hilary Ross, the wife of Wilbur Ross, Mr. Trump's commerce secretary and a frequent dinner guest of the Trumps', said in an interview. "And if her son is happy, she is happy."

Her son, who attends school in Maryland, was not in the Rose Garden as Mrs. Trump delivered her remarks. At the close of her speech, Mrs. Trump called her husband to the podium to sign a proclamation declaring May 7 "Be Best" day.

"Mr. President?" she asked.

Mr. Trump took the stage and signed the proclamation. After proudly showing off his scrawled presidential order to the crowd, the president reached for his wife and kissed her on the cheek. Mrs. Trump accepted the kiss, then automatically turned her head and offered him her other cheek.

JULIE HIRSCHFELD DAVIS contributed reporting.

CHAPTER 5

Cyberbullying and the Law

Nothing about the cyberbullying issue is simple, but how it intersects with law may be the most complicated aspect. Where does one draw the line between common drama between young adults and actual harassment? Can it be proven that a slew of unkind comments lead directly to a suicide? There's often more than one answer, and the path to justice curves. This chapter investigates.

Charges Dropped in Cyberbullying Death, but Sheriff Isn't Backing Down

BY LIZETTE ALVAREZ | NOV. 21, 2013

MIAMI — In both word and deed, Sheriff Grady Judd of Polk County has long approached crime fighting as a moral quest, a clear-cut fight between good and evil, with no-nonsense punishments for offenders.

A church-going Baptist who has been handily re-elected twice, Sheriff Judd has battled prostitution and pornography and spearheaded an effort to shutter every sex-related business in the county in Central Florida. He gave away the jail yard's basketball hoops because "if you want to play basketball, stay out of jail," as he once said, and put a stop to buying underwear for inmates. At the moment, his office is in court over its treatment of juveniles in detention, one of many lawsuits he has faced over suspected civil rights violations.

But on Wednesday, his latest effort to root out wrongdoers — this time, child cyberbullies — came unraveled. Polk County prosecutors decided to drop felony charges against two girls in a September cyberbullying case that the police said contributed to the death of 12-year-old Rebecca Ann Sedwick, who jumped from a cement plant tower two months ago.

The decision was made by the Polk County state attorney's office after weeks of investigation and an analysis of thousands of Facebook messages failed to turn up enough evidence to charge the girls, one 14 and the other 12.

While the messages revealed that the 14-year-old had insulted Rebecca and called her ugly names, the kind of bullying that some children could find emotionally crushing, the posts did not rise to the level of a crime, lawyers for the two girls said.

The New York Times had not identified the girls because they are juveniles, but one, Katelyn Roman, now 13, said in an interview on NBC's "Today" show on Thursday that she had done nothing wrong.

While commending the prosecutor, Jose Baez, the lawyer for the 12-year-old girl, called it "outrageous" that Sheriff Judd arrested the girls in October, releasing their names and photographs — which appeared on national television — without evidence to support criminal charges. The girls, he said, were vilified.

Katelyn, he said, had had no contact with Rebecca since December, when the two girls, once best friends, had a fight and their friendship crumbled. In fact, the postings show that Mr. Baez's client had also been bullied.

"He wants to get up there and act like a crusader, and this time it was at the expense of two girls," Mr. Baez, who also represented Casey Anthony, the Orlando woman acquitted two years ago of murdering her toddler, said of Sherriff Judd. "They had zero by way of evidence."

Experts in bullying said it is difficult to bring charges in cyberbullying cases like Rebecca's because multiple factors are often at play in a suicide. The police and lawyers said Rebecca was a fragile girl who had a troubled home life, had been cutting herself and was ordered to go to a psychiatric facility to get help last December.

The laws on the books are not always written to deal with the nuances of cyberbullying, and the laws, so far, have had little impact on changing behavior, they said. Insults and goading online, depending on their severity, do not typically merit felony charges. "How can we prove that posts and content led to someone directly taking their own life?" said Sameer Hinduja, a criminal justice professor at Florida Atlantic University and co-director of the Cyberbullying Research Center. "The vast majority of the kids that have taken their own lives have other elements that have been pretty major."

Brian Haas, a spokesman for the state attorney's office, said prosecutors could not comment because of laws protecting juveniles.

Sheriff Judd defended his actions on Wednesday, saying that he had had enough probable cause to make an arrest and that it was up to prosecutors to decide whether to proceed. And under Florida law, law enforcement officials are allowed to release the names and photographs of juveniles charged with felonies.

Sheriff Judd said he had no regrets over his handling of the case, adding that the arrests brought attention to the growing threat of cyberbullying and its corrosive effects on children. The two girls, he said, wound up getting the help they needed.

"We've raised awareness and we've helped kids," the sheriff told reporters, adding, "I'm glad we did what we did, and we would do it again tomorrow."

But that reaction drew criticism from Katelyn's family, the girls' lawyers and Sheriff Judd's critics, who said it was damaging to the children. The arrests of the two girls in October, one month into the investigation, took even the state attorney's office by surprise, said Andrea DeMichael, a lawyer for the 14-year-old.

Lawrence Walters, a First Amendment lawyer who has sued Sheriff Judd and his office a number of times, said: "That is the misuse of the criminal justice system. You don't bring felony charges against a 12-year-old to raise awareness of a social issue, especially if there is not a valid basis for those charges."

Emilio Roman, Katelyn's father, said his family had been hounded after the arrests. His daughter was expelled from school; the family had to fight to get her back in. He and his family had also been threatened and insulted.

"They had nothing whatsoever," Mr. Roman said of the sheriff's office. "My daughter had had a fight with the girl a year ago, and then there was no contact with her."

Critics say the sheriff, who has a strong, loyal following, allows his personal agenda to drive him to use questionable tactics against suspects, including people who visit prostitutes and pornographers.

Lawyers who have challenged him in court said his office has a pattern of overcharging defendants or using racketeering laws to force defendants into a plea, a settlement or simply out of town. The sheriff has a particular fondness for sting operations to thwart prostitution.

By his own account, Sheriff Judd, who regularly trumpets his successes, has long fancied himself as a cross between two fictional sheriffs — the genial common-sense sheriff of Mayberry played by Andy Griffith, and Matt Dillon, a moral touchstone in the "Gunsmoke" town he oversees.

Sheriff Judd does not apologize for his tactics, zeal or plain-spoken words, which he views as an antidote to a culture of political correctness. When asked several years ago why a man who had killed a deputy was shot 68 times by officers who fired 110 rounds, he replied, "That's all the ammunition they had."

Others see him as a version of Joe Arpaio, the controversial Arizona sheriff with a similarly tough approach to criminals and also illegal immigrants. It is a comparison he mostly enjoys.

Asked in 2011 by the website CorrectionsOne whether he minds the controversy, his answer was unequivocal.

"It's only controversial for the people who don't understand 'real America,' " he said. "Those are the hard-working, God-fearing people who built this country who understand what's right is right and what's wrong is wrong."

Private Moment Made Public, Then a Fatal Jump

BY LISA W. FODERARO | SEPT. 29, 2010

IT STARTED WITH a Twitter message on Sept. 19: "Roommate asked for the room till midnight. I went into molly's room and turned on my webcam. I saw him making out with a dude. Yay."

That night, the authorities say, the Rutgers University student who sent the message used a camera in his dormitory room to stream the roommate's intimate encounter live on the Internet.

And three days later, the roommate who had been surreptitiously broadcast — Tyler Clementi, an 18-year-old freshman and an accomplished violinist — jumped from the George Washington Bridge into the Hudson River in an apparent suicide.

The Sept. 22 death, details of which the authorities disclosed on Wednesday, was the latest by a young American that followed the online posting of hurtful material. The news came on the same day that Rutgers kicked off a two-year, campuswide project to teach the importance of civility, with special attention to the use and abuse of new technology.

Those who knew Mr. Clementi — on the Rutgers campus in Piscataway, N.J., at his North Jersey high school and in a community orchestra — were anguished by the circumstances surrounding his death, describing him as an intensely devoted musician who was sweet and shy.

"It's really awful, especially in New York and in the 21st century," said Arkady Leytush, artistic director of the Ridgewood Symphony Orchestra, where Mr. Clementi played since his freshman year in high school. "It's so painful. He was very friendly and had very good potential."

The Middlesex County prosecutor's office said Mr. Clementi's roommate, Dharun Ravi, 18, of Plainsboro, N.J., and another classmate,

Molly Wei, 18, of Princeton Junction, N.J., had each been charged with two counts of invasion of privacy for using "the camera to view and transmit a live image" of Mr. Clementi. The most serious charges carry a maximum sentence of five years.

Mr. Ravi was charged with two additional counts of invasion of privacy for trying a similar live feed on the Internet on Sept. 21, the day before the suicide. A spokesman for the prosecutor's office, James O'Neill, said the investigation was continuing, but he declined to "speculate on additional charges."

Steven Goldstein, chairman of the gay rights group Garden State Equality, said Wednesday that he considered the death a hate crime. "We are sickened that anyone in our society, such as the students allegedly responsible for making the surreptitious video, might consider destroying others' lives as a sport," he said in a statement.

At the end of the inaugural event for the university's "Project Civility" campaign on Wednesday, nearly 100 demonstrators gathered outside the student center, where the president spoke. They chanted, "Civility without safety — over our queer bodies!"

It is unclear what Mr. Clementi's sexual orientation was; classmates say he mostly kept to himself. Danielle Birnbohm, a freshman who lived across the hall from him in Davidson Hall, said that when a counselor asked how many students had known Mr. Clementi, only 3 students out of 50 raised their hands.

But Mr. Clementi displayed a favorite quotation on his Facebook page, from the song "I'll Never Fall in Love Again": "What do you get when you kiss a guy? You get enough germs to catch pneumonia."

And his roommate's Twitter message makes plain that Mr. Ravi believed that Mr. Clementi was gay.

A later message from Mr. Ravi appeared to make reference to the second attempt to broadcast Mr. Clementi. "Anyone with iChat," he wrote on Sept. 21, "I dare you to video chat me between the hours of 9:30 and 12. Yes, it's happening again."

Ms. Birnbohm said Mr. Ravi had said the initial broadcast was an accident — that he viewed the encounter after dialing his own computer from another room in the dorm. It was not immediately known how or when Mr. Clementi learned what his roommate had done. But Ms. Birnbohm said the episode quickly became the subject of gossip in the dormitory.

Mr. Clementi's family issued a statement on Wednesday confirming the suicide and pledging cooperation with the criminal investigation. "Tyler was a fine young man, and a distinguished musician," the statement read. "The family is heartbroken beyond words."

The Star-Ledger of Newark reported that Mr. Clementi posted a note on his Facebook page the day of his death: "Jumping off the gw bridge sorry." Friends and strangers have turned the page into a memorial.

Witnesses told the police they saw a man jump off the bridge just before 9 p.m. on Sept. 22, said Paul J. Browne, the New York Police Department's chief spokesman.

Officers discovered a wallet there with Mr. Clementi's identification, Mr. Browne said.

The police said Wednesday night that they had found the body of a young man in the Hudson north of the bridge and were trying to identify it.

Officials at Ridgewood High School, where Mr. Clementi graduated in June, last week alerted parents of current students that his family had reported him missing and encouraged students to take advantage of counseling at the school.

The timing of the news was almost uncanny, coinciding with the start of "Project Civility" at Rutgers, the state university of New Jersey. Long in the planning, the campaign will involve panel discussions, lectures, workshops and other events to raise awareness about the importance of respect, compassion and courtesy in everyday interactions.

Events scheduled for this fall include a workshop for students and administrators on residential life on campus and a panel discussion titled "Uncivil Gadgets? Changing Technologies and Civil Behavior."

Rutgers officials would not say whether the two suspects had been suspended. But in a statement late Wednesday, the university's president, Richard L. McCormick, said, "If the charges are true, these actions gravely violate the university's standards of decency and humanity." At the kickoff event for the civility campaign, Mr. McCormick made an oblique reference to the case, saying, "It is more clear than ever that we need strongly to reassert our call for civility and responsibility for each other."

Mr. Ravi was freed on $25,000 bail, and Ms. Wei was released on her own recognizance. The lawyer for Mr. Ravi, Steven D. Altman, declined to comment on the accusations. A phone message left at the offices of Ms. Wei's lawyer was not returned.

Some students on the Busch campus in Piscataway seemed dazed by the turn of events, remembering their last glimpse of Mr. Clementi. Thomas Jung, 19, shared a music stand with Mr. Clementi in the Rutgers Symphony Orchestra.

On Wednesday afternoon, hours before Mr. Clementi's death, the two rehearsed works by Berlioz and Beethoven. "He loved music," Mr. Jung said. "He was very dedicated. I couldn't tell if anything was wrong."

Reporting was contributed by **AL BAKER**, **BARBARA GRAY**, **NATE SCHWEBER** and **TIM STELLOH**.

Christie Signs Tougher Law on Bullying in Schools

BY RICHARD PÉREZ-PEÑA | JAN. 6, 2011

NEW JERSEY ON THURSDAY enacted the nation's toughest law against bullying and harassment in schools, three and a half months after the suicide of a Rutgers University student drew national attention to the issue.

The law spells out a long list of requirements, including the appointment of specific people in each school and district to run antibullying programs; the investigation of any episodes starting within a day after they occur; and training for teachers, administrators and school board members. Superintendents must make public reports twice a year detailing any episodes in each school, and each school will receive a letter grade to be posted on its Web site.

The law, which goes into effect at the start of the next school year, lists harassment, intimidation or bullying as grounds for suspension or even expulsion from school. It applies to public schools, and portions of it apply to public colleges.

A bill had been in the works since 2009, but it gained momentum last fall. It passed both houses of the Legislature on Nov. 22, with just one dissenting vote, and Gov. Chris Christie signed it into law on Thursday. The New Jersey School Boards Association endorsed the law, concluding that schools could largely carry it out with existing resources.

"This is one of the great civil rights laws in New Jersey history, and to have a fairly conservative Republican governor sign it sends a resounding signal to other states," said Steven Goldstein, chairman and chief executive of Garden State Equality, a gay rights group, who was involved in drafting the law. "It's also a major achievement for bipartisan governance in New Jersey."

On Sept. 22, Tyler Clementi, a freshman at Rutgers, jumped to his death from the George Washington Bridge; three days earlier, officials have said, his roommate surreptitiously streamed video of him in an intimate encounter with another man. While it remains unclear what role the video may have played in Mr. Clementi's suicide, news coverage of the episode gave added impetus to efforts to enact laws against bullying and harassment.

"No question, that tragedy and a string of other suicides in the fall by school kids gave it momentum," said State Senator Barbara Buono, Democrat of Middlesex County, a prime sponsor of the bill. "The idea is just to make the climate of school one of tolerance and respect."

Forty-five states have laws against bullying, and New Jersey has had one since 2002, including a 2007 amendment covering cyberbullying. New Jersey becomes the fifth state to adopt a new law in the past year; New York was among the others.

"Other states have bits and pieces of what this New Jersey law has, but none of them is as broad, getting to this level of detail, and requiring them, step by step, to do the right thing for students," said Sarah Warbelow, state legislative director at the Human Rights Campaign, a national gay rights group. Many states, she said, do not even offer the protections of the 2002 New Jersey law, which made it a crime to bully or harass on the basis of race, sex, sexual and gender identity or disability.

Jury Finds Spying in Rutgers Dorm Was a Hate Crime

BY KATE ZERNIKE | MARCH 16, 2012

NEW BRUNSWICK, N.J. — A former Rutgers University student was convicted on Friday on all 15 charges he had faced for using a webcam to spy on his roommate having sex with another man, a verdict poised to broaden the definition of hate crimes in an era when laws have not kept up with evolving technology.

"It's a watershed moment, because it says youth is not immunity," said Marcellus A. McRae, a former federal prosecutor now in private practice.

The student, Dharun Ravi, had sent out Twitter and text messages encouraging others to watch. His roommate, Tyler Clementi, jumped to his death from the George Washington Bridge three days after the webcam viewing, three weeks into their freshman year in September 2010.

The case set off a debate about whether hate-crime statutes are the best way to deal with bullying. While Mr. Ravi was not charged with Mr. Clementi's death, some legal experts argued that he was being punished for it, and that this would result only in ruining another young life. They, along with Mr. Ravi's lawyers, had argued that the case was criminalizing simple boorish behavior.

But Bruce J. Kaplan, the prosecutor in Middlesex County, applauded the jury for sending a strong message against bias. "They felt the pain of Tyler," he said.

Mr. Ravi, 20, wearing a dark suit over his slight frame, sat expressionless as the jury forewoman read the verdict on the first count, of invasion of privacy. But he seemed surprised when she pronounced him guilty on the next charge, of bias intimidation. His eyes popped and he quickly turned his head from the jury. As he left the courtroom in a swarm of television cameras, his mother clutching his arm, he looked straight ahead and said nothing.

The jury also found him guilty of lying to investigators, trying to influence a witness and tampering with evidence after he tried to cover up Twitter and text messages inviting others to join in the viewing.

Some of the charges carry penalties of 5 to 10 years in prison. Mr. Ravi has surrendered his passport; prosecutors said he could face possible deportation to his native India, but that decision would be left to immigration officials. Judge Glenn Berman set sentencing for May 21.

The case was a rare one in which almost none of the facts were in dispute. Mr. Ravi's lawyers agreed that he had set up a webcam on his computer, and had then gone into a friend's room and viewed Mr. Clementi kissing a man he met a few weeks earlier on a Web site for gay men. He sent Twitter and text messages urging others to watch when Mr. Clementi invited the man again two nights later, then deleted messages after Mr. Clementi killed himself.

That account had been established by a long trail of electronic evidence — from Twitter feeds and cellphone records, dormitory surveillance cameras, dining hall swipe cards and a "net flow" analysis showing when and how computers in the dormitory connected.

What the jury had to decide, and what set off debate outside as well as inside the courtroom, was what Mr. Ravi and Mr. Clementi were thinking.

Had Mr. Ravi set up the webcam because he had a pretty good idea that he would see Mr. Clementi in an intimate moment? Had he targeted Mr. Clementi and the man he was with because they were gay? And had Mr. Clementi been in fear?

Without Mr. Clementi to speak for himself, that last question was perhaps the most difficult to determine, and jurors struggled with it.

"That was the hardest because you really can't get into someone's head," said one, Bruno Ferreira, as he left the court. The jury deliberated longest — for well more than an hour, he said — on the bias intimidation charge.

Mr. Ferreira said he ultimately voted guilty on the bias intimidation charge because Mr. Ravi had sent multiple Twitter messages about Mr. Clementi. "They were being done twice, not just one day," he said.

Another juror, Kashad Leverett, himself a student and a Twitter user, said he could relate to Mr. Ravi's constant stream of Twitter and text messages.

But the defense's insistence that Mr. Ravi had set up the webcam because he was afraid Mr. Clementi's visitor would steal something, he said, rang hollow.

"If I knew someone was going to steal something from me, I would definitely take it with me," Mr. Leverett said, adding, "Just from the fact of the second incident, it seemed that it was intentional."

The jury of seven women and five men deliberated for 13 hours over 3 days after 13 days of testimony.

Reflecting the difficulty of defining hate crimes, it had taken the judge more than an hour simply to instruct the jury on the questions they had to answer to reach a verdict.

The jury concluded that Mr. Ravi had not knowingly or purposely intimidated the men when he watched the first time, on Sept. 19, 2010.

But it found him guilty of the charge because Mr. Clementi "reasonably believed" he had been made a target because he was gay.

The prosecution had pointed out that Mr. Clementi had checked Mr. Ravi's Twitter feed — where Mr. Ravi told others he had seen his roommate "kissing a dude" — 38 times in the days after the first webcam viewing. Records showed that Mr. Clementi had gone online to request a room change, and a resident assistant testified that Mr. Clementi had complained to him.

Mr. Clementi's parents, Joe and Jane, attended the trial each day, sitting in the front row and showing little emotion.

After the verdict, Joe Clementi, the director of public works in the northern New Jersey town of Hawthorne, read a brief statement, saying the trial had been "painful for us, as it would be for any parent who must sit and listen to people talk about bad and inappropriate things that were done to their child."

Mostly, he said, he wanted to deliver a message to middle- and high-school students.

"You're going to meet a lot of people in your lifetime," he said. "Some of these people you may not like. Just because you don't like them doesn't mean you have to work against them. When you see somebody doing something wrong, tell them: 'That's not right. Stop it.' The change you want to see in the world begins with you."

Mr. Clementi's suicide came up only in passing during the trial. Still, the death defined the trial, turning what might have been a peeping Tom case or, as the resident assistant said, "a roommate issue" into something far more grave.

The testimony painted a picture of two college freshmen, both from top-performing high schools in well-off suburbs, who could not have been more different. Mr. Clementi was shy and awkward, an accomplished violinist who had only recently told his parents he was gay. Mr. Ravi was popular but boastful, a computer wizard and ultimate Frisbee player who communicated with friends constantly via Twitter, text message and iChat.

Mr. Ravi's parents, who brought him here from India when he was young, sat vigil behind him each day, with a large group of friends, including several who had served as character witnesses for Mr. Ravi, testifying he was not biased against gay people.

Mr. Ravi had rejected plea deals, because prosecutors would have required him to admit to bias intimidation. His lawyers said he simply did not believe he had committed a hate crime. They argued that he was "a kid" with little experience of homosexuality who had stumbled into a situation that scared him.

His lead lawyer, Steven Altman, made only a brief statement via e-mail following the verdict, saying "rest assured" he would appeal.

Gay rights advocates, who had used the example of Mr. Clementi's suicide to push New Jersey to pass what is considered the nation's toughest antibullying law, hailed the jury's decision.

"This verdict sends the important message that a 'kids will be kids' defense is no excuse to bully another student," said Steven Goldstein, the chairman of Garden State Equality.

Mr. Kaplan, the county prosecutor, rejected suggestions that Mr. Ravi would not have been on trial if Mr. Clementi had not killed himself. Even if he had not, he said, "under these facts, under this evidence, we would prosecute this case."

WILLIAM GLABERSON and **DAVID M. HALBFINGER** contributed reporting from New York, and **NATE SCHWEBER** from New Brunswick.

Rutgers Webcam-Spying Defendant Is Sentenced to 30-Day Jail Term

BY KATE ZERNIKE | MAY 21, 2012

NEW BRUNSWICK, N.J. — A judge here sentenced Dharun Ravi to 30 days in jail on Monday for using a webcam to spy on his roommate having sex with a man, a punishment that angered prosecutors and did little to quiet the debate over using laws against hate crimes to fight antigay bias.

His roommate, Tyler Clementi, killed himself in September 2010, two days after discovering that Mr. Ravi had spied on him in their room at Rutgers University, galvanizing national concern about suicide among gay teenagers.

Mr. Ravi had faced up to 10 years in prison after a jury convicted him of all 15 counts against him, which included bias intimidation, invasion of privacy and tampering with a witness and evidence.

Prosecutors vowed to appeal, and the sentence surprised even many who had called for leniency, as it came after an extended scolding by Judge Glenn Berman in Superior Court in Middlesex County.

"I heard this jury say guilty 288 times — 24 questions, 12 jurors, that's the multiplication," the judge told Mr. Ravi, recalling the questionnaire jurors filled out in arriving at the verdict. "And I haven't heard you apologize once."

"I do not believe he hated Tyler Clementi," the judge told a courtroom packed on one side with supporters of Mr. Ravi and on the other with those of the Clementi family. "I do believe he acted out of colossal insensitivity."

Prosecutors and Mr. Clementi's family, who had addressed reporters with relief bordering on buoyancy following the verdict two months ago, canceled a news conference planned for after the sentencing. Mr. Ravi's family collapsed into an embrace with his lawyers. Just moments earlier, his mother, Sabitha Ravi, had sobbed while imploring the judge to spare her son prison time.

"The media misconstrued the facts to the public and misconceptions were formed," she said, telling how she watched helplessly as her son sank into despair after he was charged and dropped out of Rutgers, barely eating or leaving the house. "All I could do was hug him and cry."

At her tears, Mr. Ravi himself broke down crying, the first time since the beginning of the trial that he had publicly shown more than a glimpse of emotion.

Mr. Ravi, 20, was not charged with causing Mr. Clementi's death, but the suicide hung heavily over the trial, and over the sentencing on Monday. Mr. Clementi's mother, father and brother spoke before the judge delivered his decision, breaking down occasionally as they recalled his accomplishment and his promise, and the pain of losing him and of reliving the agony of his final days as they endured three weeks of courtroom testimony.

"I cannot imagine the level of rejection, isolation and disdain he must have felt from his peers," Tyler's brother James Clementi said. "Dharun never bothered to care about the harm he was doing to my brother's heart and mind. My family has never heard an apology, an acknowledgment of any wrongdoing."

His mother, Jane Clementi, also criticized students who knew about the spying from Mr. Ravi's Twitter feeds. "How could they all go along with such meanness?" she said. "Why didn't any one of them speak up and try to stop it?"

Judge Berman said he wanted to impose a sentence that was "constructive" and would provide a measure of closure — "though I don't know how the Clementis will ever get closure," he said. He said he imposed the jail time for witness and evidence tampering and for lying to the police. But for the bias intimidation convictions, he gave Mr. Ravi three years' probation.

The judge did not explicitly say why he deviated so far from the maximum sentence. But he said he believed the State Legislature had intended prison time to be attached to crimes of violence, and there had been none.

Mr. Ravi's lead lawyer, Steven Altman, had earlier read from a presentencing memo by a corrections officer who had interviewed Mr. Ravi and recommended against incarceration.

Mr. Ravi, who came to this country from India as a child, remains a felon and could face deportation. But the judge said he would recommend against that.

Gillian M. Christensen, a spokeswoman for Immigration and Customs Enforcement, said the agency was "in the process of reviewing documents relating to the conviction and sentencing" of Mr. Ravi, but would not comment further.

Some immigration lawyers pointed on Monday to a clause declaring that a legal resident, or green card holder, like Mr. Ravi can be deported if convicted of two or more crimes involving "moral turpitude," as long as neither crime arose out of a single scheme.

Thomas E. Moseley, an immigration lawyer based in Newark, said that if the immigration authorities "wanted to be really aggressive," they might argue that the tampering crime was separate from the bias crime.

Judge Berman also sentenced Mr. Ravi to 300 hours of community service, counseling about cyberbullying and what he called "alternate lifestyles," and approximately $11,000 in fees. Most of the money is to be used to help victims of bias crimes.

Mr. Clementi, an 18-year-old who had recently come out to his parents, and Mr. Ravi were three weeks into their freshman year at Rutgers when Mr. Clementi asked if he could have the room for the evening so he could be alone with a man, whom he had met on a Web site for gay men.

In court, prosecutors presented a long trail of electronic evidence to show how Mr. Ravi had set up a webcam to spy on the men, then gone into a friend's room and watched. He caught only a glimpse of Mr. Clementi and his visitor in an embrace, then sent out Twitter messages announcing that he had seen his roommate "making out with a dude." He set up the camera again two days later and urged others to watch.

But by then, Mr. Clementi had seen the Twitter posts and turned off the webcam.

Mr. Clementi, an accomplished violinist from Ridgewood, N.J., checked Mr. Ravi's Twitter feed 38 times and filed a request for a room change — and then jumped to his death from the George Washington Bridge. In court on Monday, his mother said she feared Mr. Ravi's Twitter posts were the last thing her son saw before he jumped.

Many gay rights advocates had hailed the jury's verdict as a bold strike against bias, a message that bullying of gay men and lesbians should not be dismissed as a mere prank.

But other prominent gay commentators argued that while what Mr. Ravi did was repugnant, it was not the kind of sustained or aggressive behavior that constitutes bullying.

The sentence similarly divided them.

Steven Goldstein, the chairman of Garden State Equality, a New Jersey gay rights group that pushed for the state to pass its strict antibullying statutes after Mr. Clementi's death, said the sentence was lighter than what many shoplifters received.

"We have opposed throwing the book at Dharun Ravi," Mr. Goldstein said in a statement. "But we have similarly rejected the other extreme, that Ravi should have gotten no jail time at all, and today's sentencing is closer to that extreme than the other."

William Dobbs, who had attended rallies supporting Mr. Ravi, said the judge was reflecting the discomfort many gay rights campaigners expressed at the use of hate crimes to prosecute Mr. Ravi.

"The judge had to control a backlash to an out-of-control prosecution," he said. "The number of charges, the severity and the potential penalties, even the amount of resources devoted to this trial, was out of all proportion to the incident."

Bruce J. Kaplan, the Middlesex County prosecutor, issued a statement after the sentencing, saying that while his office had not requested the maximum prison term, "it was expected that his conviction on multiple offenses of invading the privacy of two victims on two separate occasions, four counts of bias intimidation against Tyler Clementi, and the cover-up of those crimes would warrant more than a 30-day jail term."

Still, even some jurors continued to struggle over the appropriate sentence. One, Susan Matiejunas, said she had watched the proceedings on television all morning and was surprised.

"Thirty days is a slap on the wrist," she said. "Six months to a year would have been more suitable, since we convicted him on so many counts."

Ms. Matiejunas telephoned later to say she had reconsidered.

"The kid has spent two years in purgatory just waiting for all of this to end," she said. "I think probably 30 days really is quite enough on top of all that."

NATE SCHWEBER contributed reporting from New Brunswick, and **HANNAH MIET** and **KIRK SEMPLE** from New York.

When Neighbors Tangle Online

BY RONDA KAYSEN | NOV. 6, 2015

COMPLAINING ABOUT THE co-op or condominium board is practically a blood sport in New York, an unfortunate side effect of living under the rule of elected volunteers. Usually, disputes go no further than a heated exchange at the annual meeting. Much like a family feud, the dirty laundry is rarely aired in public. But thanks to the Internet, that is changing.

At two Brooklyn co-ops, for example, disgruntled residents have launched publicly accessible websites critical of board members and how their buildings are managed. In response, board members at both buildings have filed defamation lawsuits against the shareholders.

When such disputes leave the building, even residents who have nothing to do with the board or the website can be affected. If a building's reputation is publicly marred, property values can suffer. Buyers might reconsider making an offer if a cursory web search turns up a catalog of misery and misfortune.

"Social media has given people more platforms to speak their minds, especially since they can do it behind closed doors — they don't have to face the people that they're arguing with," said Stacey R. Patterson, a real estate lawyer who represents condos and co-ops in New York and New Jersey. "Between chat rooms and Facebook pages, you set up anything and you can start a war."

"It's just starting," said Dean M. Roberts, the corporate counsel for Trump Village Section 4, a 1,144-unit complex in Coney Island, Brooklyn. "As more buildings get a web presence and people generally become more web aware, you're going to start having your dissident fights on the Internet."

At Trump Village Section 4, conflict between shareholders and building management went public three years ago when residents launched a website, TV4 United or TV4News.org. Last year, the

EMON HASSAN FOR THE NEW YORK TIMES

Igor Oberman, a former president of Trump Village Section 4 in Brooklyn, is suing some residents for defamation.

building and Igor Oberman, who was then president of its board, sued Julia Bezvoleva and Inna Yeselson, along with seven others who used pseudonyms, for defamation. Among the John Doe defendants was "Josef Stalin," who posted comments like, "Why we let a dirty no good politicians [sic] destroy our investment?" according to court documents.

In August, a judge ruled that the case had enough merit to proceed, dismissing the defense's argument that a board member is a public figure. For a public figure to sue for defamation, he or she must prove that the critic knew that the information was inaccurate and had malicious intent. The hurdle for proving defamation is lower for private citizens.

Trump Village Section 4 was built in 1964 by Donald J. Trump's father, Fred C. Trump. Today, a three-bedroom apartment there sells for around $450,000, according to a real estate agent who is familiar with the buildings.

Search the web for the building's name and TV4News.org immediately pops up, with dozens of posts critical of Mr. Oberman, who is, like many of the residents, a native of the former Soviet Union.

One such post questions the merits of an article published in a building newsletter about a canceled carnival. "The fact that this newspaper is totally controlled by Mr. Oberman is reminiscent of communism," it reads. "It makes us wonder, who is the communist using KGB tactics?"

Mr. Oberman, critics say, ran the complex with an iron fist. "I don't know what his problem is, but he just doesn't like people who don't agree with him," said Eugene Ovsishcher, 45, a Trump Village resident who is not part of the suit. Mr. Ovsishcher successfully fought an eviction suit a few years ago that was sparked by his need for an emotional support dog, a Shih Tzu, at a time when the complex prohibited pets.

The Department of Housing and Urban Development stepped into the fray in January, charging Mr. Oberman and Trump Village Section 4 with discrimination against Mr. Ovsishcher and his wife. The case has since been referred to a federal prosecutor.

Mr. Oberman says the board has gone out of its way to comply with HUD rules. Board members have gone through HUD training and the building has changed its pet policy to allow for pets.

Although the language can be heated, TV4News does raise legitimate issues. Lengthy posts question board election tactics, inspection rules and eviction policies. Jim Quinn, a lawyer representing the two named defendants, who deny involvement in the website, said he believes the lawsuit is intended to silence critics. "If you lived in a building and you thought that someone was mishandling the building," he said, "you would want to talk about it."

Mr. Oberman maintains that his critics represent a handful of shareholders unhappy with his methods, such as using drones to search for unregistered air-conditioners in windows. "Whenever you try to enforce rules you have a lot of people who say it's not fair," he said. As for elections, he said, the board uses outside vendors to handle ballots.

In the past, if residents wanted to fight a board, they had to find a time and place to meet. But with a website, aggrieved neighbors can commiserate 24/7.

"If somebody is doing something that is wrong and you can share that experience with somebody else, you can talk yourself down from the ledge," said Justin W. Patchin, a director of the Cyberbullying Research Center. "But there is also the concern of the mob mentality."

And websites can be misleading. A site rife with outraged comments could represent the thoughts and opinions of dozens of residents or it could be a platform for one loud voice.

"What do you do when Ms. O'Leary, the crazy cat woman in 5C, starts putting up these postings and you're trying to sell your apartment?" Mr. Roberts said. "It's hard to delineate the truthfulness of some Internet stuff because crazy cat woman's comments look the same as the board president's comments."

These days, even business review sites like Yelp are rife with posts critical of various apartment complexes. Some buildings are playing offense with management-sanctioned chat rooms on platforms like BuildingLink.com.

Even the tamest of online forums can turn testy.

"You have a lot of keyboard warriors," said Douglas Lee, 33, a member of a Google Group at the Edge, a condo in Williamsburg, Brooklyn.

"We have to remember that just because you're reading it on the Internet doesn't mean that it doesn't hurt," said Sherry Turkle, the author of "Reclaiming Conversation: The Power of Talk in a Digital Age" (Penguin, 2015). "Face-to-face conversation is work. Getting back to it is work, but it's work that we know how to do and it's work worth doing."

For the targets of online attacks, the emotional fallout takes its toll. Friends, business associates and relatives frequently ask Mr. Oberman, 42, about TV4News, he said. Potential shareholders have inquired about it at board interviews, he said.

“Being a punching bag is one thing,” said Mr. Oberman, who resigned from his post as board president in June to take a paid position as the complex’s property manager. “Being hung, quartered and crucified is different.”

An Internet search of Mr. Oberman’s name pulls up TV4News first, followed by articles about the HUD investigation and the $7,500 fine Mr. Oberman received last year from the city’s Conflicts of Interest Board over campaign violations made when he ran unsuccessfully for the City Council. But Mr. Oberman, who is appealing the board’s decision, said the other negative press did not carry the same personal sting. The website “is basically saying we’re crooks and we’re cooking the books,” Mr. Oberman said. “I think that’s very upsetting.”

Mr. Oberman says that because of his critics, he plans to sell his three-bedroom and move to Staten Island.

Brokers who sell at Trump Village 4 suspect the fracas has dissuaded some buyers.

“I’ve had good sales there, but could I have had better sales? Could I have had more buyers? I don’t know,” said John Cerrone, a salesman at Douglas Elliman. “To say that people are openly expressing dissatisfaction and to say that cannot have an effect, I think that’s naïve.”

On a website about 2800 Coyle Street, a co-op in Sheepshead Bay, Brooklyn, residents are divided into two groups: “Good Guys” and “Bad Guys.”

Topping the list of “bad guys” is Svetlana Marmer, who has been president of the co-op board for eight years and owns two apartments in the 157-unit building. She is described on the site as “a bitter woman who is angry that she has achieved nothing in life.”

The contents of the website, along with emails sent by shareholders to residents and outside recipients, convinced Ms. Marmer and two other board members to sue five named shareholders and two anonymous defendants for defamation in 2013.

“To be president, it’s not easy,” Ms. Marmer, 69, said. “Believe me, it’s not easy.”

EMON HASSAN FOR THE NEW YORK TIMES

A pier near the Edge, in Williamsburg, Brooklyn, where revelers annoyed members of a resident Google Group.

Judging by the website, the animosity in the building predates Hurricane Sandy, which had a severe impact on 2800 Coyle Street, where peeling paint and crumbling plaster have yet to be remedied. And the damage wrought by the storm escalated an already contentious situation.

"It's a disaster, it's like a homeless shelter," said Vadim German, 54, a defendant in the defamation suit, whose ground-floor apartment sustained $29,000 in damages from the storm.

Dissatisfied residents of 2800 Coyle Street accuse management of not making necessary repairs after the storm, compounding long-standing claims of corruption, mismanagement and engaging in a pattern of intimidation.

Alec Sauchik, the co-op's corporate council, argues that the real victims are the board members who have been repeatedly criticized and harassed for doing their job, including trying to make building repairs. "There's been a witch hunt going on for almost a decade by a small group of individuals who were essentially trying to unseat the board," Mr. Sauchik said.

Mr. German said he did not know who created the website. He said he did write emails critical of the leadership. "If I call the president of the company a pirate, I don't know if it's slander," he said. "If it's true, why is it slander?"

Mr. Sauchik declined to say why his clients believe the defendants created the website.

Not all online forums degenerate into battle mode. At the Edge, the condo in Williamsburg, residents started the Google Group in 2011, a year after the development opened. Initially, they used the email listserv to vent about the challenges of living in new construction — How do you make the refrigerator stop chirping?

Residents did not have control over the condo board (and still do not), so the forum provided space to discuss issues away from the watchful eye of the sponsor.

Dennis Lin, one of the original members, has administered it almost since the beginning, reading every email residents write. He has never removed a post, but he has weighed in when tempers flare.

"A lot of times when I say, 'Let me find out more,' it calms everybody down," said Mr. Lin, who is 38 and works in finance.

Now, the group has more than 600 members, all owners. Renters cannot join, nor can residents of the affordable housing component of the Edge next door. Membership is by invitation from an existing or former member. Mr. Lin approves requests by confirming ownership through city records.

Members use the group to ask neighbors to water their plants, to sell their wares and to organize parties. But it is also used to address problems, giving members a platform to organize so that they have a larger voice in the building and the neighborhood than they might have otherwise.

When residents had complaints about the garage, alleging scratched cars and slow service, Mr. Lin collected photographs and stories of incidents, delivering 17 pages of evidence to the parking management company.

And when members were bothered by people making noise along the public waterfront at night, members coordinated calls to 311 and collected photographs of the goings-on. Last year, Mr. Lin, who is now a member of the condo board, and other building representatives met with the local City Council member, the Parks Department and the Police Department about noise concerns.

Most members seem to understand that, in a complex where a penthouse recently sold for $3.812 million, airing grievances can have consequences.

"People are aware that even though this is a private, invitation-only group, emails are emails and they could get forwarded to anybody," Mr. Lin said. But ultimately, the benefits outweigh the risks. "We are a community," he said. "We have a huge benefit by having this group."

Glossary

anonymous-sharing apps Smartphone apps, such as Secret and Yik Yak, that allow anonymous sharing of information among Internet users.

bot A web robot that performs automated tasks on the Internet.

bullying Using intimidation or ridicule to inflict pain on others or to control others' actions.

#ClickWithCompassion A hashtag campaign developed by Monica Lewinsky and her public relations team to help combat cyberbullying and support victims of online harassment.

coercive Related to using threats or force to persuade someone do something.

community moderators People who monitor comments on various websites and social media for offensive or harmful content. They can settle disputes, remove content that breaks a forum's rules and properly categorize comments depending on the site and the extent of the moderator's capabilities.

Conversation AI A tool developed by the Google subsidiary Jigsaw that uses machine learning to identify harassment online.

cyberbullying Bullying on the Internet or via text. Also referred to as online harassment.

DeepText An algorithm used to detect bullying comments on Instagram that determines how words are used in a similar way to the human brain.

defamation The act of spreading false statements about someone to hurt their reputation.

hack To gain access to someone else's computer files without their permission.

harassment The act of creating an unpleasant or hostile situation for someone.

profile Display of personal facts linked with a specific computer user.

resilient Able to recover quickly from difficult circumstances.

rumor Unsubstantiated information that may or may not be true.

screenshot A saved copy of what appears on a computer's or smartphone's screen at a certain time.

slander To make a false spoken statement that leads others to have a bad opinion of someone.

stigma A negative and often unfair set of beliefs associated with something.

subpoena A written command requiring a person to produce documents or to appear in court.

troll Internet user who thrives on provoking negative reactions from other users, via online abuse and harassment. Also known as a cyberbully.

Media Literacy Terms

"Media literacy" refers to the ability to access, understand, critically assess and create media. The following terms are important components of media literacy, and they will help you critically engage with the articles in this title.

angle The aspect of a news story that a journalist focuses on and develops.

attribution The method by which a source is identified or by which facts and information are assigned to the person who provided them.

balance Principle of journalism that both perspectives of an argument should be presented in a fair way.

bias A disposition of prejudice in favor of a certain idea, person or perspective.

byline Name of the writer, usually placed between the headline and the story.

caption Identifying copy for a picture; also called a legend or cutline.

chronological order Method of writing a story presenting the details of the story in the order in which they occurred.

column A type of story that is a regular feature, often on a recurring topic, written by the same journalist, generally known as a columnist.

commentary A type of story that is an expression of opinion on recent events by a journalist generally known as a commentator.

credibility The quality of being trustworthy and believable, said of a journalistic source.

critical review A type of story that describes an event or work of art, such as a theater performance, film, concert, book, restaurant, radio or television program, exhibition or musical piece, and offers critical assessment of its quality and reception.

editorial Article of opinion or interpretation.

fake news A fictional or made-up story presented in the style of a legitimate news story, intended to deceive readers; also commonly used to criticize legitimate news because of its perspective or unfavorable coverage of a subject.

feature story Article designed to entertain as well as to inform.

headline Type, usually 18 point or larger, used to introduce a story.

human interest story A type of story that focuses on individuals and how events or issues affect their lives, generally offering a sense of relatability to the reader.

impartiality Principle of journalism that a story should not reflect a journalist's bias and should contain balance.

intention The motive or reason behind something, such as the publication of a news story.

interview story A type of story in which the facts are gathered primarily by interviewing another person or persons.

inverted pyramid A method of writing a story using facts in order of importance, beginning with a lead and then gradually adding paragraphs in order of relevance from most interesting to least interesting.

motive The reason behind something, such as the publication of a news story or a source's perspective on an issue.

news story An article or style of expository writing that reports news, generally in a straightforward fashion and without editorial comment.

op-ed An opinion piece that reflects a prominent individual's opinion on a topic of interest.

paraphrase The summary of an individual's words, with attribution, rather than a direct quotation of their exact words.

plagiarism An attempt to pass another person's work as one's own without attribution.

quotation The use of an individual's exact words indicated by the use of quotation marks and proper attribution.

reliability The quality of being dependable and accurate, said of a journalistic source.

rhetorical device Technique in writing intending to persuade the reader or communicate a message from a certain perspective.

source The origin of the information reported in journalism.

sports reporting A type of story that reports on sporting events or topics related to sports.

style A distinctive use of language in writing or speech; also a news or publishing organization's rules for consistent use of language with regards to spelling, punctuation, typography and capitalization, usually regimented by a house style guide.

tone A manner of expression in writing or speech.

Media Literacy Questions

1. Identify the various sources cited in the article "Online Bullies Pull Schools Into the Fray" (on page 144). How does Jan Hoffman attribute information to each of these sources in her article? How effective are Hoffman's attributions in helping the reader identify her sources?

2. In "The Ornithologist the Internet Called a Murderer" (on page 59), Kirk Wallace Johnson directly quotes Dr. Christopher Filardi. What are the strengths of the use of a direct quote as opposed to a paraphrase? What are the weaknesses?

3. Compare the headlines of "Monica Lewinsky Is Back, but This Time It's on Her Terms" (on page 45) and "Monica Lewinsky Breaks Her Public Silence With a TED Talk" (on page 56). Which is a more compelling headline, and why? How could the less compelling headline be changed to better draw the reader's interest?

4. What type of story is "Letting Your Kids Play in the Social Media Sandbox" (on page 121)? Can you identify another article in this collection that is the same type of story?

5. Does Lizette Alvarez demonstrate the journalistic principle of impartiality in her article "Charges Dropped in Cyberbullying Death, but Sheriff Isn't Backing Down" (on page 179)? If so, how did she do so? If not, what could she have included to make the article more impartial?

6. The article "Secret's Doomed Script" (on page 76) is an example of an op-ed. Identify how Joe Nocera's attitude and tone help convey his opinion on the topic.

7. Does "Private Moment Made Public, Then a Fatal Jump" (on page 184) use multiple sources? What are the strengths of using multiple sources in a journalistic piece? What are the weaknesses of relying heavily on only one source or a few sources?

8. "The Rise of the Internet Fan Bully" (on page 66) features a photograph. What does this photograph add to the article?

9. What is the intention of the article "Harassed Online, She Remains Determined to Enlist in the Marines" (on page 36)? How effectively does it achieve its intended purpose?

10. Analyze the authors' reporting in "Who Spewed That Abuse? Anonymous Yik Yak App Isn't Telling" (on page 79) and "In Rise of Yik Yak App, Profits and Ethics Collide" (on page 92). Do you think one journalist is more balanced in their reporting than the other? If so, why do you think so?

Citations

All citations in this list are formatted according to the Modern Language Association's (MLA) style guide.

BOOK CITATION

THE NEW YORK TIMES EDITORIAL STAFF. *Cyberbullying: A Deadly Trend.* New York: New York Times Educational Publishing, 2019.

ONLINE ARTICLE CITATIONS

ALVAREZ, LIZETTE. "Charges Dropped in Cyberbullying Death, but Sheriff Isn't Backing Down." *The New York Times*, 21 Nov. 2013, https://www.nytimes.com/2013/11/22/us/charges-dropped-against-florida-girls-accused-in-cyberbullying-death.html.

ALVAREZ, LIZETTE. "Girl's Suicide Points to Rise in Apps Used by Cyberbullies." *The New York Times*, 13 Sept. 2013, https://www.nytimes.com/2013/09/14/us/suicide-of-girl-after-bullying-raises-worries-on-web-sites.html.

BAZELON, EMILY. "Defining Bullying Down." *The New York Times*, 11 Mar. 2013, https://www.nytimes.com/2013/03/12/opinion/defining-bullying-down.html.

BELSON, KEN. "Ex-Dolphin Jonathan Martin Is Detained After Social Media Post Shuts School." *The New York Times*, 23 Feb. 2018, https://www.nytimes.com/2018/02/23/sports/football/jonathan-martin.html.

BENNETT, JESSICA. "Monica Lewinsky Breaks Her Public Silence With a TED Talk." *The New York Times*, 19 Mar. 2015, https://www.nytimes.com/2015/03/22/fashion/monica-lewinsky-ted-talk.html.

BENNETT, JESSICA. "Monica Lewinsky Is Back, but This Time It's on Her Terms." *The New York Times*, 19 Mar. 2015, https://www.nytimes.com/2015/03/22/style/monica-lewinsky-is-back-but-this-time-its-on-her-terms.html.

BILTON, NICK. "Letting Your Kids Play in the Social Media Sandbox." *The New York Times*, 18 Feb. 2015, https://www.nytimes.com/2015/02/19/style/letting-your-kids-play-in-the-social-media-sandbox.html.

BILTON, NICK. "Meet Facebook's Mr. Nice." *The New York Times*, 22 Oct. 2014, https://www.nytimes.com/2014/10/23/fashion/Facebook-Arturo-Bejar-Creating-Empathy-Among-Cyberbullying.html.

BILTON, NICK. "Name-Calling in the Virtual Playground." *The New York Times*, 23 Mar. 2014, https://bits.blogs.nytimes.com/2014/03/23/name-calling-in-the-virtual-playground/.

BROMWICH, JONAH ENGEL. "Hackers Publish Nude Pictures on Leslie Jones's Website." *The New York Times*, 24 Aug. 2016, https://www.nytimes.com/2016/08/25/movies/leslie-jones-website-hacked.html.

COHAN, WILLIAM D. "In Rise of Yik Yak App, Profits and Ethics Collide." *The New York Times*, 7 Apr. 2015, https://www.nytimes.com/2015/04/08/business/dealbook/profits-and-ethics-collide-in-nameless-turmoil.html.

ECKHOLM, ERIK, AND KATIE ZEZIMA. "Questions for School on Bullying and a Suicide." *The New York Times*, 1 Apr. 2010, https://www.nytimes.com/2010/04/02/us/02bully.html.

FODERARO, LISA W. "Private Moment Made Public, Then a Fatal Jump." *The New York Times*, 29 Sept. 2010, https://www.nytimes.com/2010/09/30/nyregion/30suicide.html.

HESS, AMANDA. "The Rise of the Internet Fan Bully." *The New York Times*, 12 Aug. 2016, https://www.nytimes.com/2016/08/15/arts/music/the-rise-of-the-internet-fan-bully.html.

HOFFMAN, JAN. "As Bullies Go Digital, Parents Play Catch-Up." *The New York Times*, 4 Dec. 2010, https://www.nytimes.com/2010/12/05/us/05bully.html.

HOFFMAN, JAN. "Online Bullies Pull Schools into the Fray." *The New York Times*, 27 June 2010, https://www.nytimes.com/2010/06/28/style/28bully.html.

HOLSON, LAURA. "Instagram Unveils a Bully Filter." *The New York Times*, 1 May 2018, https://www.nytimes.com/2018/05/01/technology/instagram-bully-filter.html.

ISAAC, MIKE. "A Founder of Secret, the Anonymous Social App, Is Shutting It Down." *The New York Times*, 29 Apr. 2015, https://www.nytimes.com/2015/04/30/technology/a-founder-of-secret-the-anonymous-social-app-shuts-it-down-as-use-declines.html.

JOHNSON, KIRK WALLACE. "The Ornithologist the Internet Called a Murderer." *The New York Times*, 15 June 2018, https://www.nytimes.com/2018/06/15/opinion/sunday/moustached-kingfisher-internet-harassment.html.

KAYSEN, RONDA. "When Neighbors Tangle Online." *The New York Times*, 8 Nov. 2015, https://www.nytimes.com/2015/11/08/realestate/when-neighbors-tangle-online.html.

KLASS, PERRI, M.D. "In the Fight Against Bullying, a Glimmer of Hope." *The New York Times*, 28 Aug. 2017, https://www.nytimes.com/2017/08/28/well/family/in-the-fight-against-bullying-a-glimmer-of-hope.html.

MAAG, CHRISTOPHER. "When the Bullies Turned Faceless." *The New York Times*, 16 Dec. 2007, https://www.nytimes.com/2007/12/16/fashion/16meangirls.html.

MAHLER, JONATHAN. "Who Spewed That Abuse? Anonymous Yik Yak App Isn't Telling." *The New York Times*, 8 Mar. 2015, https://www.nytimes.com/2015/03/09/technology/popular-yik-yak-app-confers-anonymity-and-delivers-abuse.html.

NOCERA, JOE. "Secret's Doomed Script." *The New York Times*, 5 May 2015, https://www.nytimes.com/2015/05/05/opinion/joe-nocera-secrets-doomed-script.html.

NORTH, ANNA. "Can Bots Fight Bullying?" *The New York Times*, 21 Sept. 2016, https://takingnote.blogs.nytimes.com/2016/09/21/can-bots-fight-bullying/.

PARKER-POPE, TARA. "More Teens Victimized by Cyber-Bullies." *The New York Times*, 27 Nov. 2007, https://well.blogs.nytimes.com/2007/11/27/more-teens-victimized-by-cyber-bullies/.

PARKER-POPE, TARA. "When Your Child Is the Cyberbully." *The New York Times*, 29 June 2010, https://well.blogs.nytimes.com/2010/06/29/when-your-child-is-the-cyberbully/.

PÉREZ-PEÑA, RICHARD. "Christie Signs Tougher Law on Bullying in Schools." *The New York Times*, 6 Jan. 2011, https://www.nytimes.com/2011/01/07/nyregion/07bully.html.

PHILIPPS, DAVE. "Harassed Online, She Remains Determined to Enlist in the Marines." *The New York Times*, 14 Mar. 2017, https://www.nytimes.com/2017/03/14/us/harassed-online-she-remains-determined-to-enlist-in-the-marines.html.

Rogers, Katie. "Melania Trump Rolls Out 'Be Best,' a Children's Agenda With a Focus on Social Media." *The New York Times*, 7 May 2018, https://www.nytimes.com/2018/05/07/us/politics/melania-trump-children.html.

Rogers, Katie. "Melania Trump Wants to End Online Bullying. Her Husband Doesn't Help." *The New York Times*, 20 Mar. 2018, https://www.nytimes.com/2018/03/20/us/politics/trump-melania-bullying-cybersafety.html.

Rogers, Katie, and Jonah Engel Bromwich. "Hackers Publish Nude Pictures on Leslie Jones's Website." *The New York Times*, 24 Aug. 2016, https://www.nytimes.com/2016/08/25/movies/leslie-jones-website-hacked.html.

Rozsa, Lori. "Spying on College Life, via Yik Yak." *The New York Times*, 11 Jan. 2015, https://parenting.blogs.nytimes.com/2015/01/11/spying-on-college-life-via-yik-yak/.

Safronova, Valeriya. "The Rise and Fall of Yik Yak, the Anonymous Messaging App." *The New York Times*, 27 May 2017, https://www.nytimes.com/2017/05/27/style/yik-yak-bullying-mary-washington.html.

Sandomir, Richard. "Curt Schilling Off Little League Broadcasts After 'Unacceptable' Tweet." *The New York Times*, 25 Aug. 2015, https://www.nytimes.com/2015/08/26/sports/baseball/curt-schilling-off-little-league-broadcast-after-unacceptable-tweet.html.

Sengupta, Somini. "Warily, Schools Watch Students on the Internet." *The New York Times*, 28 Oct. 2013, https://www.nytimes.com/2013/10/29/technology/some-schools-extend-surveillance-of-students-beyond-campus.html.

Silva, Daniella. "Bieber Fights Cyberbullies, but It Wasn't His Idea." *The New York Times*, 10 Oct. 2012, https://cityroom.blogs.nytimes.com/2012/10/10/justin-bieber-makes-cyberbullying-video-to-get-associates-out-of-trouble/.

Suaya, Stacy. "An App Combats Bullying, One Anonymous Compliment at a Time." *The New York Times*, 20 Dec. 2016, https://www.nytimes.com/2016/12/20/fashion/austin-kevitch-brighten-app-anti-bullying.html.

Wayne, Teddy. "Found on Facebook: Empathy." *The New York Times*, 11 Oct. 2015, https://www.nytimes.com/2015/10/11/fashion/found-on-facebook-empathy.html.

White, Martha C. "How Do You Stop Bullying? Advertisers Try to Help." *The New York Times*, 29 Oct. 2017, https://www.nytimes.com/2017/10/29/business/media/monica-lewinsky-bullying-ad.html.

WINGFIELD, NICK. "Survey Exposes Prevalence of Online Harassment." *The New York Times*, 22 Oct. 2014, https://bits.blogs.nytimes.com/2014/10/22/survey-exposes-prevalence-of-online-harassment/.

ZERNIKE, KATE. "Jury Finds Spying in Rutgers Dorm Was a Hate Crime." *The New York Times*, 16 Mar. 2012, https://www.nytimes.com/2012/03/17/nyregion/defendant-guilty-in-rutgers-case.html.

ZERNIKE, KATE. "Rutgers Webcam-Spying Defendant Is Sentenced to 30-Day Jail Term." *The New York Times*, 21 May 2012, https://www.nytimes.com/2012/05/22/nyregion/rutgers-spying-defendant-sentenced-to-30-days-in-jail.html.

Index

A

Aboujaoude, Elias, 86
Adamson, Allen, 42, 44
Ad Council, 42
Adesman, Andrew, 24, 25
Aftab, Parry, 130, 149
Aiken, Mary, 71
Alloway, Tracy, 111
Altman, Steven, 187, 193, 197
Andreessen, Marc, 73, 77
Arthur, Heidi, 42, 43

B

Bader-Wechseler, Chrys, 72–75, 77, 78, 103, 105
Baez, Jose, 180
Barrymore, Drew, 112–113
"Be Best" program, 174–178
Be Cool Be Nice, 107
Bejar, Arturo, 118–120
Bekoff, Marc, 60
Belmont, Veronica, 103
Berman, Glenn, 191, 195, 196, 197
Bieber, Justin, 27–28
Billingsley, Anna, 100
Blau, Brian, 74
Boisselle, Edward J., 164
Brackett, Marc, 119, 120
Bradshaw, Catherine, 23, 24
Braun, Scott, 27–28
Brennan, Thomas, 38
Brighten, 9, 106–107
Brunault, Brian, 130, 131, 133
Buffington, Brooks, 82, 83, 84, 86, 88, 92, 96, 98
Buono, Barbara, 189
Byttow, David, 72–75, 77, 78, 103

C

Cabello, Camila, 67–69
Carter, Cris, 29–30
Christie, Chris, 188–189
Citron, Danielle Keats, 54, 81
Clementi, Joe, 192–193
Clementi, Tyler, 52, 184–187, 188–189, 190–194
Collier, Anne, 140
Coloroso, Barbara, 167
Conversation AI, 9, 70–71
Conway, Kellyanne, 174
Crouch, Margaret, 79
Cuddy, Amy, 58
Cunningham, Savannah, 36–40

D

Darrow-Rioux, Jana, 164
DeepText, 9
DiFebo, Val, 43
Dobbs, William, 198
Domenech, Daniel A., 160
Douglas, Gabby, 34
Droll, Tyler, 82, 83, 84, 85, 86, 92, 96, 98
Durand, Aaron, 103

E

Elena, Justine, 39
Ellis, Ross, 42, 99
Englander, Elizabeth K., 125–128, 131, 132, 136, 141, 153

F

Facebook, 30, 36, 59, 61, 64, 66, 73, 74, 80, 82, 83, 90, 92, 94, 106, 108–111, 113, 115, 116, 118–120, 123, 126, 127, 129, 131, 132, 133, 135, 136, 139, 141, 147, 148, 149, 150, 153, 154, 155, 156, 157, 158, 159, 160, 161, 168, 180, 185, 186, 200
Facefeed, 104
Facing History School, 142–143
Feig, Paul, 34
Fifth Harmony, 66–69
Filardi, Christopher, 59–65
Friend, David, 48, 53
Frydrych, Chris, 160–161

G

Geo Listening, 160, 161
Gillibrand, Kirsten, 37
Goetz, Jim, 86, 93–95
Goldstein, Steven, 185, 188,

194, 198
Google, 9, 70, 74, 168
Green, Ronald L., 38
Grisham, Stephanie, 173, 175–176
Guerra, Nancy G., 11

H

Hahn, Greg, 41, 43
Hess, Amanda, 57
Hinduja, Sameer, 34
Hines, Morgan, 101, 102
Hurley, Richard, 96, 99

I

Instagram, 9, 31, 32, 36, 94, 112–113, 116, 118, 123, 124
Instagram DeepText, 9, 113
Ivester, Matt, 83

J

James, Bernard, 153, 155
Jenner, Kendall, 107
Jigsaw, 9, 70
Johnson, Myeshia, 170
Jones, David, 161
Jones, Leslie, 33–35, 66, 67, 68
Judd, Ashley, 57
Judd, Grady, 179–183
Judge, Mike, 76, 78
JuicyCampus, 83

K

Kaplan, Bruce J., 190, 194, 198–199
Katz, Debra, 96, 100
Keltner, Dacher, 120
Kevitch, Austin, 9, 106–107
Kind Campaign, 107
Kordei, Normani, 66–69

L

LaPorta, James, 38
Leff, Stephen, 24, 25, 26
Letterman, David, 49
Lewinsky, Monica, 9, 41, 43, 45–55, 56–58

M

Maher, Bill, 49
Mahler, Jonathan, 93
Malik, Zayn, 69
Martin, Jonathan, 31
McAdam, Mary Ann, 155
McCormick, Richard L., 187
McQuaide, Hilary, 95
McRae, Marcellus A., 190
Meier, Megan, 12–16, 126
Mullen, Matthew, 84, 97
Musick, Kelli, 99, 100, 101

N

Neller, Robert B., 37
Newton, Karina, 113

O

Oberman, Igor, 201, 202, 203, 204
O'Brien, Colleen, 60
O'Brien, Darby, 164
Ohanian, Alexis, 73
One Direction, 69
O'Neill, Bailey, 20, 21
Opferman, Susan, 104
Orsini, Tony, 144, 146, 147, 150, 154, 156, 157
Oswalt, Patton, 34

P

Palfrey, John G., Jr., 161–162
Park, Hunter M., 97
Patchin, Justin, 14
Pediatrics, study published by, 23–26
Perry, Katy, 34
Pew Research Center study, 17–19
Prince, Phoebe, 126, 164–168

Q

Questlove, 33

R

Rafferty, Mike, 145
Ravi, Dharun, 184, 185, 186, 187, 190–194, 195–199
"Reclaiming Conversation," 109
Rhimes, Shonda, 58
Rice, Kathleen M., 28
Roberts, Walter, 15
Roman, Emilio, 182
Roman, Katelyn, 180, 181, 182
Roppo, James, 27–28
Rose, Amber, 112
Rosen, Larry D., 109, 110, 140
Ross, Hilary, 178

S

Sacca, Chris, 58
Sayer, Gus, 163, 165
Scheibel, Elizabeth D., 163, 165
Schilling, Curt, 29–30
school policies, 11, 23–26, 144–158, 159–162, 163–167, 188–189
Secret, 9, 70, 72–75, 76–78, 80, 103–105, 123
Sedwick, Rebecca Ann, 114–117, 180–183
Seman, Jordan, 85, 86, 96
Shahidi, John, 104
Shanks, Nelson, 50
Shirky, Clay, 54
Shots, 104

"Silicon Valley," 76, 77
Smith, Susan, 165
Smith, Willow, 107
Snapchat, 34, 124
Socia, Deb, 155
Steinem, Gloria, 53
Stoetzel, Kelly, 51
suicide, 9, 12, 13, 15, 20, 25, 31, 32, 103, 114–117, 145, 159, 160, 163–167, 179, 180, 181, 184, 185, 186, 188, 189, 190, 193, 195, 196
Systrom, Kevin, 112, 113

T

Taylor, Jeff, 149, 155
Telegram, 123
Terebin, Ilja, 104, 105
Todd, Amanda, 20, 21
Traister, Rebecca, 49
Trestan, Robert O., 29
Trump, Donald, 168–173, 174–178
Trump, Melania, 168–173, 174–178
Turkle, Sherry, 108, 203
Twitter, 28, 29, 30, 33, 34, 51, 57, 59, 64, 66, 67, 68, 69, 73, 74, 80, 82, 90, 93, 101, 111, 113, 116, 118, 123, 159, 160, 161, 168–173, 174, 184, 185, 190, 191, 192, 193, 196, 197, 198
Tynes, Brendesha, 34, 35

W

Walters, Barbara, 49, 53, 54
Walters, Lawrence, 181–182
Warbelow, Sarah, 189
Wearley, Meredith, 147, 148, 150
Wei, Molly, 185, 187
West, Lindy, 57
Whisper, 73, 80
Wiles, Leon, 86
Williams, Kirk R., 11
Winarsky, Norman, 71
Wu, Greg, 146, 147, 154, 158

Y

Yik Yak, 9, 70, 73, 75, 78, 79–88, 89–91, 92–95, 96–102, 104, 123
YouTube, 28, 65, 77, 94, 111, 113, 121, 123, 124, 145, 151, 152

Z

Zoberman, Maxwell, 86–87

This book is current up until the time of printing. For the most up-to-date reporting, visit www.nytimes.com.